'Bedtime,' she said to Thomas.

His chubby little arms wrapped around her and he returned her hug, nestling his head against her shoulder.

'I love you, Sophie,' he said. 'And I love Aunt Etty, and I love Gib.'

Sophie glanced towards Gib, to see how he'd taken this declaration, and caught a strange expression in his eyes.

Or maybe his eyes looked perfectly normal; it was the subdued lighting from the pool that made them look—

Not sad, exactly.

Then he took two long strides towards them and planted a kiss on Thomas's cheek.

'Goodnight, little man,' he said, and then he touched Sophie on the head.

'Goodnight to you, too,' he added, huskily enough for Sophie to know that they would probably have done more tonight than watch the river glide by…

TOP-NOTCH DOCS

He's not just the boss,
he's the best there is!

These heroes aren't just doctors,
they're life-savers.

These heroes aren't just surgeons,
they're skilled masters.
Their talent and reputations are admired by all.

These heroes are devoted to their patients.
They'll hold the littlest baby in their arms,
and melt the hearts of all who see.

These heroes aren't just medical professionals,
they're the men of your dreams.

He's not just the boss,
he's the best there is!

A FATHER BY CHRISTMAS

BY
MEREDITH WEBBER

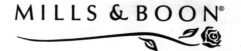

MILLS & BOON®

All the characters in this book have no existence outside the imagination of the author, and have no relation whatsoever to anyone bearing the same name or names. They are not even distantly inspired by any individual known or unknown to the author, and all the incidents are pure invention.

First published in Great Britain 2006
Harlequin Mills & Boon Limited,
Eton House, 18-24 Paradise Road, Richmond, Surrey TW9 1SR

© Meredith Webber 2006

ISBN-13: 978 0 263 84774 1
ISBN-10:   0 263 84774 8

Set in Times Roman 10½ on 12¾ pt
03-1206-48689

Printed and bound in Spain
by Litografia Rosés, S.A., Barcelona

A FATHER BY CHRISTMAS

Meredith Webber says of herself, 'Some years ago, I read an article which suggested that Mills & Boon® were looking for new medical authors. I had one of those "I can do that" moments, and gave it a try. What began as a challenge has become an obsession, though I do temper the "butt on seat" career of writing with dirty but healthy outdoor pursuits, fossicking through the Australian Outback in search of gold or opals. Having had some success in all of these endeavours, I now consider I've found the perfect lifestyle.'

Recent titles by the same author:

BRIDE AT BAY HOSPITAL
THE DOCTOR'S MARRIAGE WISH
  Crocodile Creek: 24-Hour Rescue
SHEIKH SURGEON
COMING HOME FOR CHRISTMAS

CHAPTER ONE

SOPHIE had been so hell-bent on finding Thomas's father that the one thing she should have considered hadn't occurred to her. Not until two forty-seven on a Wednesday afternoon while she was wandering through the mall in Brisbane, trying not to think about Thomas and how he might be handling his new child-care situation—trying not to worry...

Then, from nowhere, it slammed into her mind—the question she'd never considered. The 'what if his father has changed his mind and wants him' question that hadn't, until that precise moment, entered her head.

She was seized by panic so strong that she had to steady herself with one hand against a jeweller's window. Breathing deeply, she told herself the father, whoever he turned out to be, didn't even know Thomas existed, so of course he wouldn't want him.

Telling herself lies?

'It will be OK!' she muttered, saying the words over and over under her breath as if repetition might make them stronger.

'Are you all right?'

An elderly woman stopped beside her and one glance

at the kind but anxious face was enough to pull Sophie out of her shock.

'Yes, thank you,' she said, aware she must look very far from all right for the stranger to have stopped. 'Just felt a little faint.'

'There's a book store on the next corner with a great coffee shop on the ground floor,' her good Samaritan said. 'I find wandering through book stores wonderfully therapeutic.'

Sophie had to smile.

'Me, too,' she replied. 'Thank you for telling me about it.'

She moved cautiously away from the window, pleased to find the weakness gone, her brain functioning again and her legs obeying the order to move. She didn't need a coffee, but she'd buy a book for Thomas...

'Mum and Dad, Aunt Etty, the Pritchards and Marilyn. Mum and Dad, Aunt Etty, the Pritchards and Marilyn.'

Gib was still repeating the names as he stared blankly at the rows and rows of books in front of him. It had become a meaningless mantra. He was too tired to be doing this—too tired for his brain to function effectively.

'Go home and get some sleep,' his receptionist had said. Not, 'Go do your Christmas shopping!'

Maybe he should have listened!

But if not now, when? The two members of his team currently in hospital wouldn't be back any time soon and finding locum paediatricians with neonatal experience this close to Christmas, when the world and his wife were off on holiday, was like finding...well, snow on the ground outside, here in midsummer in sunny Queensland.

'Having any luck?'

He was reciting the list of the 'must get' presents once

more under his breath when the deep, smoky words penetrated his exhaustion.

Turned to see dark smoky eyes that exactly matched the voice.

The jolt of recognition he felt startled him, although he couldn't say for certain he knew the tall, ebony-haired woman standing on the other side of a low carousel of cookery books.

'Not much,' he said, seeing a frown that probably matched his own gathering between her fine black eyebrows.

'Me neither,' she said, waving her hand towards the array of brightly coloured covers in front of her. 'But, then, I'm not really trying, just filling in time.'

Her frown was still firmly in place, and he was pretty sure his was, too, the recognition signals annoyingly persistent.

'Do I know you?'

They spoke together, the chorused words bringing a flash of a smile to her face, lightening it for a moment—making it beautiful.

Or was exhaustion creating fantasies in his head?

Not in hers, apparently, for she was holding out her hand—saying her name.

'Sophie Fisher.'

'Sophie Fisher? *Dr* Sophie Fisher?'

He took her hand and held it, seeing not this tall, slim woman in jeans and a faded T-shirt, long dark hair escaping from a knot of some kind at the back of her head, but a poised, elegant woman in a black suit, dark hair swept carefully back into a neat pleat.

'*My* Dr Fisher?'

He was sounding like an idiot but his beleaguered brain was having trouble making the leap between the two women.

And her hand was twitching in his as she tried to tug it free.

'I thought you would still be in Sydney.'

'Dr Gibson?'

His name was hesitant on her lips and her frown had deepened, but her brain was obviously working better than his for she got in the first apology.

'I'm sorry. I should have recognised you at once from the interview. Blame preoccupation. It's Thomas's first full day at the hospital child-care centre—he's had three morning sessions to get used to the place, but this was all day, and I've been seriously stressed. I thought I'd fill in the day house-hunting but that's an exercise in frustration. Apparently accommodation near the hospital doesn't become available until the new year, when staff transfers occur. More stress!'

Her gabbled explanation and faltering smile betrayed the truth of her statement. She pushed straying hair back from her face with long, slim fingers as she added, 'Book stores seem to offer refuge, don't they?'

He remembered noticing her hands—beautiful hands—when she'd reached across the table to take the folder of information his secretary had prepared for the three candidates. Remembered being surprised he'd noticed because it had been so long since he'd noticed anything in particular about any woman...

'I'm sorry!' Was he repeating himself now? 'I'm standing here like a malfunctioning robot. In fact, that might just about describe me. We're—'

He broke off as another—far better—thought struck him.

'You were looking for a house? Thomas has started at the child-care centre? You're already here to stay?'

He grasped her by the arm and led her towards the escalator.

'Coffee,' he said. 'I passed a coffee shop on the ground floor. We'll talk over coffee.'

As a distraction from her own anxious thoughts, the man's appearance was a blessing, but did she need a madman as team boss? Sophie eyed Dr Alexander Gibson warily as he hauled her onto the escalator. He'd looked and acted quite normal when she'd been interviewed—clean-shaven, neat hair, dark suit and tie, very proper!—but perhaps that had been a front for the other members of the interviewing panel.

Aware, however, that one should humour madmen, she went with him, studying the flecks of silver showing in his dark hair, thinking, absurdly, that he needed a haircut.

Did his wife not remind him?

And why had she noticed his wedding ring?

'I'm sorry, you must think I'm crazy.'

He accompanied this new apology with a charming smile as he turned to steady her as she stepped off the escalator, but the smile failed to hide neither the deep lines of exhaustion in his face, visible beneath the rough stubble on his chin nor the dark shadows beneath his red-rimmed blue eyes.

Without conscious thought, she lifted her hand towards him, then realised she'd been about to touch his cheek and quickly withdrew it, covering the weird movement with a question.

'Rough time?'

Gib saw her frown return and eyes, which he'd thought brown but now saw were grey, darken. Had he flinched as her hand had moved towards him?

The way his nerves were it was only too likely, but rather than apologise again, he simply steered her towards the coffee shop, dumped her at a table and strode to the counter to place their order.

Their order? He hadn't asked.

'*Lattè*,' she said, not dumped at all but right beside him. 'And a slice of that poppy seed cake, please.'

He realised, belatedly, she was talking to the girl behind the till, and though he protested as Sophie passed across the correct change, she ignored him, simply taking a table number and returning to where he'd thought he'd left her.

'Long black, same table number,' he said to the girl, then felt the heat of embarrassment as he turned away, only to be reminded he hadn't paid. So, by the time he returned to where Dr Sophie Fisher was sitting placidly at the table and sat down opposite her, he was wondering if asking her— begging her—to start work early was as good an idea as it had seemed, up there between biography and cooking.

'So?' she said, and smiled again. And again he registered beautiful. Though when the smile faded he looked hard at her face and saw that though she had great bones and a strong, individual kind of face, it was at best attractive.

As in attracting him? The idea was so bizarre he simply stared at her.

'You wanted to speak to me, Dr Gibson?' she eventually prompted, growing more certain by the moment the man had something seriously wrong with him. Now he was staring at her—not in a man-looking-at-a-woman kind of way, but intently, as if trying to see beneath her skin and bones and into her brain.

Maybe *she* had something wrong with *her*! Something more than first-whole-day-at-child-care and what-if-his-father-wants-him worries over Thomas.

'Gib. Call me Gib. Even my patients call me Gib, those old enough to talk, of course,' he said, switching his attention from her face to the table number, which he now twisted on its stand. 'I'm not doing this too well, but I've had about six hours' sleep in the last forty-eight and I'm not functioning at one hundred per cent efficiency—probably not even fifty per cent. Then realising who you were—it seemed like a miracle.'

He looked up and met her eyes.

'I'm not that used to miracles,' he said, and although he spoke lightly, she sensed the words were painfully true.

Recently true.

'Are any of us?' she said, trying to sound offhand, although her own personal miracle—the one she'd hoped and prayed for—hadn't happened either.

'I guess not, although in paediatrics especially we do occasionally see one, don't we?'

'A badly injured baby boy who lives when he should have died? A teenage girl whose bone-marrow transplant takes? I suppose we do.'

'And now you,' he said, and smiled.

Afterwards, Sophie would wonder why the tired smile of an exhausted man should have affected her at all, but right now all she could do was stare at it, transfixed by its strength and character, although it was entirely a mouth smile, not reaching the dark shadows in his eyes—not lighting them at all.

'I'm a miracle?' she said, still seeing the smile, although it had passed only fleetingly across his face.

'You are indeed,' he told her, and smiled again, although this time at the waitress who was serving their coffees and Sophie's slice of cake.

'Are you sure you wouldn't like something to eat with your coffee?' the waitress asked, wiping nonexistent crumbs from the table and simpering at the man.

'Quite sure,' he said, but before he could smile at her again, Sophie interrupted the little bit of byplay.

'You were explaining the miracle,' she reminded him. The waitress threw her a dirty look and moved away reluctantly, while Sophie registered that underneath the tiredness and incipient beard there was a very handsome man.

He sugared his coffee and took a cautious sip, then sighed in pleasure and drained the cup, setting it down carefully in its saucer before looking at her again.

'Two of my team—my current number two, the one you'll be replacing, and a second-year resident—have recently become engaged. Usual celebrations, then driving home from visiting her parents last weekend an out-of-control truck slammed into their car and they're both in hospital.'

Pity for the young couple, injured at the peak of their happiness, swamped through Sophie.

'Are they badly hurt? Will they be all right?'

Her companion frowned though not, she thought, at her this time.

'They'll be fine, but it will take time. Petra sustained injuries to both legs and has external fixators on them, Pete has comminuted fractures of his left leg, yet to be operated on, and damage to his right shoulder that will take a series of ops to fix. Pete was driving and has internal injuries as well—damaged spleen...'

'And you're down two team members,' Sophie said, understanding now why the man looked so tired. 'But surely the other teams...'

'Three weeks before Christmas, when it seems the whole of Queensland goes on holiday? My team was the only one where none of the staff was taking Christmas leave, mainly because Pete's moving on at the end of the month and Petra's saving all her leave for her wedding next year.'

'So with two down there's you and…?'

'A second-year resident, Yui Lin. She's good, but she's not Superwoman. And I suspect she's pregnant, although she hasn't said anything, so I'm worried about pushing her too hard. Did you work through your pregnancy?'

At the interview, not wanting to go into her private life any more than she'd had to, she'd mentioned only that she had a child. Now it would be so easy to explain who Thomas was, but fear she might lose him had driven Sophie to Brisbane—well, fear and a hospital child-care centre that had a great reputation—and a shadow of that fear held her back.

'Is all this leading to a question of whether I can start work earlier?' she asked instead. 'Because, if it is, the short answer is no.'

She studied the face across the table as she delivered this blow, but if he was disappointed he showed no hint of it—and if he was surprised she hadn't answered his question there was no sign of that either.

Impassive, the face was.

Impassive, though dreadfully tired.

So dreadfully tired Sophie felt a twinge of guilt for not being willing to help out.

'And the long answer?'

She sighed.

'I came up early for a number of reasons, the first being to settle Thomas in at the hospital child-care centre before I started work. I wanted to know for certain he was OK so I wasn't worrying about him when I should be completely focussed on the job. The second thing was to find accommodation, which, apparently, is impossible this time of the year, but the third, and most important, is to find a carer of some kind—a live-in nanny, so there's someone there for Thomas when I'm on night duty or on call.'

She glanced across the table at him, wondering if he had children and would understand how important it was to find the right person. No answer in his face—the impassive look still in place.

Maybe he was asleep...

'I didn't want a full-time nanny because she'd still need time off and erratic hospital hours mean you can't count on giving someone regular time off, so the child-care centre filled daytime needs—'

'It operates at night, too, you know,' he said, proving he was at least hearing what she was saying.

'Yes, but waking a three-year-old at two in the morning, carrying him out to the car, driving him to the hospital and then dumping him in the centre is not my idea of the perfect solution! I want a granny-type person. Someone willing to live in—make her home with us—someone who loves kids and will give Thomas lots of hugs and read stories to him. Someone who'll be free to do whatever she wants during the day most of the time, but be there for him at night. Someone special in his life...'

She sighed again and when her companion didn't respond, she added, 'Realistically I know this person might not exist, but I have to try, you see. And finding someone even close to just right will take time. So, though I'd love to help out, Dr Gibson, it just isn't possible right now.'

'Gib,' he reminded her, and Sophie stared at him, wondering again if the man had the full complement of working neurones. She was telling him about her concern over finding a suitable carer for Thomas and he was insisting she call him by his nickname.

She ate some cake and drank some coffee, thinking when she'd finished both she'd leave, then realised he was smiling at her—a full, lips-spread, eyes-aglint smile that did funny things to her lungs.

'Search no longer for your granny,' he announced. 'You can have Aunt Etty!'

He sat back in his chair, the smile growing even brighter.

'Aunt Etty?'

The echo of the words was so faint Gib realised the woman was confused. He hurried to explain.

'Aunt Etty will be perfect for you. Adores children, volunteers at the child-care centre at the hospital and is bored to death living with me—says I'm never home to make a mess or cook for so what is she supposed to do?'

'But your aunt—she might not want a job.'

The woman was still confused.

'She's not my aunt, she's my wife's. Look, I've still got time. What if I run you home and you meet her and have a chat then I'll drive you to the hospital to collect Thomas? Although I'll have to go to a darned meeting, you can take your little boy back to talk to Etty to see how they both get on.'

Sophie opened her mouth to protest, but it was too late, Dr Gibson—Gib—was asking her about transport—where was her car, she *did* have a car? Or was the hospital organising one as part of her salary package?

'I brought my own car up from Sydney,' she said, swept along in the man's conversational wake, although she knew cars weren't the issue. 'It's at the hospital. I was going to catch the bus back.'

'Perfect,' her new boss announced, standing up and leaning over to take her elbow. 'Let's go!'

Which was how Sophie found herself in a quietly luxurious saloon, being driven down a road that ran alongside a wide brown river, purple jacaranda blossoms dropping from the trees that lined the road.

'You've missed the best of the jacarandas,' he said, 'but poincianas will be in flower soon—brilliant scarlet flowers making a canopy over the trees. Great for Christmas decorations—the red flowers and green leaves.'

Sophie turned to stare at him. His behaviour so far had been approaching manic yet he took the time to know and notice trees and flowers and think of Christmas decorations. He turned as if he'd read her thoughts and smiled again, lightening the rather stern profile she'd been regarding with more than a casual interest.

'Aunt Etty's mad about plants and trees and gardens.'

I won't sigh again, Sophie decided, stifling the breath of confusion. I'll just sit here and be swept along and meet Aunt Etty, and when he drops me back at the hospital I'll tell him no. At least all this is taking my mind off the Thomas's father problem!

The road left the river, winding away from it, then cut back towards it, Gib eventually pulling into a tree-shaded drive at the end of which stood a house that looked like a cottage from a child's picture book.

'We extended in the other direction so we didn't spoil the look of the place,' Gib said, and Sophie went back to frowning at him. First flowers, now this! He couldn't possibly be reading her thoughts!

Then he explained.

'Everyone seeing the house wonders about the size of

it. As a matter of fact, the extensions are far too big. We've closed off one wing completely, to cut down on housekeeping. Actually…'

He paused in his forward rush towards the house as he said the last word, and studied her consideringly for a moment—then shook his head and charged on again, Sophie following meekly in his wake, wondering if his wife was at home and, if she was, how she'd feel about Gib giving away her aunt.

Not that Sophie intended taking her…

'Come on in!'

Gib urged his new colleague forward, so excited at his own brilliance it didn't occur to him she might have reservations.

'Etty!' he called, then heard the smooth slide of rubber across the polished floorboards. 'Look what I found!'

Etty stopped her chair a few feet from them and looked from him to Sophie then back to him.

'A woman! Great! I've been telling you you should but I must say she doesn't look as delighted at being found as you obviously are at finding her. Perhaps she wasn't lost.'

She wheeled forward and put out her hand.

'I'm Etty Pritchard, and in case the head case here hasn't explained, it's spina bifida. Got around on sticks for quite a while—still can if I really have to—but the chair's the easiest and fastest.'

Gib, watching for Sophie's reaction, saw the young woman smile again, and once more registered the luminous beauty this expression brought to her face. But he should be explaining things, not watching Sophie Fisher's face. Etty, as usual, had the wrong end of the stick.

'She's my new neonatologist,' he began, but Etty wasn't listening, talking instead to Sophie who'd leaned against the wall and in so doing had unobtrusively diminished her height somewhat so Etty wasn't forced to look up quite so far.

'She needs a carer for her little boy.' Gib thought if he kept talking maybe someone would eventually listen. 'I told her you'd be ideal.'

How could he possibly have thought a woman in a wheelchair would be a suitable carer for an active little boy? Sophie wondered as she followed Aunt Etty along the passage. Then it opened into a living room and she saw the broad sweep of the river and, to the left, the tall buildings of the city centre.

'Wow!'

Etty paused and turned back towards her, turning herself and the wheelchair on the proverbial sixpence.

'Nice view?'

'Unbelievable,' Sophie said, her eyes drinking in the beauty.

'Why don't you stay here and enjoy it?' Etty suggested. 'Sit there, and I'll get us something cool to drink.'

Instead of sitting, Sophie moved towards the floor-to-ceiling windows, most of which were open to let in the river breeze. From here, she could see the garden where it stepped in terraces down to the river.

'Dr Gibson said you gardened,' she said, turning back as she heard the wheelchair approaching. 'How do you manage getting down the different levels?'

Etty handed her a tall glass filled with pale liquid, a mint leaf floating with the ice at the top.

'See over by the right side—Gib put in a lift affair. It has a ramp and all I have to do is hang on, press the button and it pulls me up or lets me down. Works like a ski-lift—one of those ones that drag you up the hill.'

Sophie shook her head in admiration then took a sip of her drink and admiration turned to astonishment.

'This tastes like homemade lemonade. I haven't had it since my grandmother died.'

Etty smiled at her.

'We've two lemon trees and both bear heavily so I've always got plenty of fruit for lemonade.'

'And lemon butter, and lemon delicious pudding, and preserved lemons and every other lemon dish you can imagine,' Gib put in, coming to join them with a tall glass of lemonade in his hand.

He's selling her too hard, Sophie thought, studying the man who now leaned against the windows and stared out at the river. Does he want to get rid of her? Is he finding it irksome to have his wife's aunt in the house all the time? Had she come as a housekeeper but now he wants more privacy?

Impossible to guess at answers. Sophie drank more of the delicious lemonade and, for a fleeting moment, considered coming home on a hot evening to a view of the river and cold, homemade lemonade…

CHAPTER TWO

'Etty, Sophie is a colleague, due to start work on my team in the new year. She's from Sydney so presumably all her contacts and family are down there. For that reason, she came up early to find accommodation, settle her little boy, Thomas, into the hospital child-care centre and to employ a live-in person to be there for Thomas when she's on night duty or on call. She was telling me what she needed and I thought of you!'

Sophie watched as Etty faced her nephew.

'Now, be honest, Gib! You thought, Great, here's someone to help out while Pete and Petra are in hospital and somehow I have to organise her life for her so she can start work as soon as possible, preferably tonight.'

Sophie hid her smile as Gib looked first taken aback, then slightly angry, then gave in and smiled.

'More or less,' he admitted, 'but I did remember you complaining about being bored and needing a new distraction in your life. What could be more distracting than a three-year-old boy?'

Etty returned his smile, and Sophie saw that though they might not be related by blood there was a strong tie of affection between the two of them.

Maybe he *was* trying to help Sophie out, not get rid of Aunt Etty from his house.

'You've been bulldozing Sophie, haven't you?' Aunt Etty accused. 'And you've put her into a very awkward position. She might not want someone like me—age, sex, whatever—minding her little boy, but if she says no now, she'll worry I'll think it's because of the wheelchair.'

'But I never gave the chair a thought,' Gib protested, and Sophie believed him. How could you consider a woman who kept a big garden on three levels as neat as his obviously was as disabled? She was probably far more capable than a lot of women her age.

And she made super lemonade.

Aware this wasn't the issue, Sophie turned to Etty.

'I don't think the problem is whether or not I would want to employ you, but why you'd want the job. You're obviously well settled here, and you have the garden, which you love. We're living in a drab serviced apartment in the city and don't look like getting anything better for another six weeks. '

'I don't think where you live is important. Have you thought about the kind of person you want to have on hand for your little boy? For Thomas?'

Etty's gently asked question made Sophie stop and think.

'I have,' she said slowly, realising the person she'd envisaged was sitting right in front of her. 'I thought a kind of granny—someone kind who hugged a lot and didn't get frustrated by the million and one questions little boys find to ask. Who understood little boys get dirty and didn't fuss too much.'

Etty held out her arms.

'Well, if you don't mind the chair, here I am,' she said. 'Gib was speaking truthfully when he said I was bored, and I'm aware for my own well-being I need a new challenge. You must have reservations about the physical side of things, but the staff at the hospital child-care centre will give me references.'

Sophie knew she had to look at references and, though an inner conviction that Etty would be the ideal live-in carer for Thomas was growing all the time, she also knew she should be asking more questions—that she should take her time to think this through and not be rushed into it.

'In the end, I would assume,' Gib offered, 'it will depend on Thomas, won't it? He might be disconcerted by someone in a wheelchair. He might not like Etty. Why don't we take her when you go to pick him up? Or, better yet, do as I suggested earlier. You could collect him and bring him back here so the two of them can spend some time together. He might like a swim.'

Sophie glanced towards the river, which was beautiful but very brown. Etty caught her concern and laughed.

'There's a pool downstairs. It's kind of indoor-outdoor so I can swim all year round.'

Gib looked towards the wing of the house he kept closed off. Just how hard would it be, having a colleague sharing his house?

He glanced towards the tall, slim woman, smiling now at Etty, so beautiful again. The real question was, how hard would it be having *this* colleague sharing his house? The fingers of his right hand found his wedding band and he twisted it round and round, even easing it towards his knuckle, wondering if he'd be able to get it off when and if he ever wanted to.

'I'll know when the time is right,' he'd said to Etty when she'd asked if he wanted to take it off.

But that had been four years ago...

* * *

They drove back towards the hospital, Etty chattering away, pointing out landmark buildings and naming the suburbs through which they passed, while Sophie studied the back of Gib's head. He'd showered and shaved back at the house, and looked more like the man who'd interviewed her, but his too long, still damp hair curled slightly at the nape of his neck, and those tiny dark curls drew Sophie's eyes with a magnetic force she found impossible to resist.

The curls or the man?

How can you think about a man when you have so many other problems to sort out?

Especially a man with a wife.

But just then, as part of a conversation she'd tuned out, he turned and smiled at her, and something in that smile curled into her chest and squeezed hard at her heart.

He had a wife!

She forgot about not sighing and let out a long breath of expired air...

He parked outside the child-care centre and climbed out of the car to get Etty's wheelchair from the boot, setting it up and wheeling it around to the passenger side of the car. Sophie watched as Etty transferred herself efficiently from one mode of transport to another then turned to—to what? Thank Gib?

She hesitated and he saved her saying anything.

'We'll talk later,' he said to Sophie, taking her hand and shaking it in a curiously formal manner that didn't stop tremors of awareness sparking along her nerves. Etty was already wheeling herself towards the centre, but Sophie watched her new boss climb back into his car and drive away, all the while wondering why a handshake should make her feel uneasy.

Although it wasn't the handshake that unsettled her, it was her own weird reaction to it.

'Oh, Dr Fisher, I was hoping you'd be late.' Vicki, the young woman in charge of Thomas's group, greeted Sophie with this strange comment, then explained, 'We had a visit from one of Santa's elves and it went longer than we expected. Thomas managed to stay awake throughout the fun but he's not long fallen asleep. Do you want to wake him or would you prefer to wait—maybe have a cup of coffee in the canteen?'

Sophie turned to Etty, intending to ask her, but the older woman was already chatting to the centre manager—chatting like old friends.

'You go and have a coffee,' Etty said to Sophie. 'I volunteer here occasionally so most of the kids know me. I'll stay and play and maybe meet Thomas that way when he wakes up.'

Sophie looked around helplessly. It felt as though her life was spinning out of control.

Would a cup of coffee help?

She didn't know where the canteen was, although she did remember a nice coffee shop off the hospital's main foyer, from when she'd been here for the interview.

Did she also remember the way to the NICU? *That* would be a far better destination. Not that she intended meekly falling in with Dr Gibson's plans and starting work earlier than had been arranged, but looking at the babies would centre her—bring her back to earth. She had her hospital ID, having organised it in order to enrol Thomas in the child-care centre. She'd visit the NICU—look at babies for a while.

* * *

Gib looked from the chart to tiny Andrew Atkins, his mind running through everything they'd already tried to relieve the baby's RDS.

'Would the mother having pre-eclampsia have made it worse?' Albert, the charge nurse who'd paged him earlier, enquired.

Gib shook his head.

'Maternal pre-eclampsia is one of the factors that's supposed to protect pre-term babies from respiratory distress syndrome,' he muttered, more to himself than to Albert. 'But what happened earlier doesn't matter now. What matters is that Andrew's getting worse when he should be getting better. He's had surfactant, he's on continuous positive airway pressure, there's no indication of infection, yet he's still labouring to breathe and it's affecting his heart.'

'Could there be a new infection?'

Gib turned as he heard the voice and frowned, not at the interruption but at the woman who shouldn't be here.

'Where's Thomas?'

'Sleeping.'

Gib nodded as if accepting the explanation, or perhaps he'd ignored it and was simply indicating the baby.

'This is Andrew. He's got RDS, and as you can see he's on continuous positive airway pressure, but he's failing. He's had a full course of ampicillin and an aminoglycoside to cover Group B strep, Listeria and gram negative organisms. His blood cultures have been negative for infection for seventy-two hours.'

Sophie moved closer and looked at the baby, small enough to fit in the palm of her hand. She'd have loved to touch him, but hadn't washed up, intending just to look.

Picking up the X-rays from the cart beside the baby's cot, she held them to the light. The lungs showed the strange 'ground-glass' appearance of the hyaline membranes— the other name for RDS being hyaline membrane disease.

'Pneumothorax?' she said to Gib, who was still staring at her as if she were a being from outer space.

'I thought it might be that—that's why I paged Gib,' the nurse explained. 'Sudden increase in BP then bradycardia and hypotension. I thought pneumothorax for sure, but you can see on the new X-rays up there in the light box, they don't show it.'

'Albert, this is Sophie Fisher, the neonatalogist who's due to join the team in January. I've been hoping to persuade her to start early and it looks…' he broke off to smile at Sophie '…as if I might have succeeded.'

Then he nodded at the baby.

'I think we'll have to put him on high-frequency ventilation. It's a shame because he's been breathing on his own so well, even though he's needed the extra oxygen. I've been trying to avoid it because once he's dependent on the ventilator we'll have to go through the process of weaning him off, then there's the added complication of air leaks. But what else can we do?'

He turned to Sophie.

'How about you stay here with Andrew while Albert sets it up? I'll tell the Atkins what's happening.' He glanced at his watch. 'It's fifteen minutes since we sent them outside, and they'll be getting anxious.'

'Anxious? They'll be paranoid,' Sophie muttered to Albert, wondering for the thousandth time just how parents of pre-term or low birth weight babies coped. The new healthy pink baby they'd imagined they'd be taking home didn't exist, and instead they had this fragile wee infant, taken from them and cocooned in a special crib, with pads and wires and murmuring monitors taking the place of loving hands, sweet songs and gentle kisses.

'Parents get it good here,' Albert said to her as he set up the ventilator. 'They've a special waiting room for times like this, and they're allowed to stay with their baby all the time, apart from shift changes and doctors' rounds. They can touch, and talk and sing, and even hold the baby once he or she is strong enough. We encourage that and ask parents to kangaroo the infant—opening their gown or shirt and holding him or her against their chest. And we've got three of those little swing-like hammocks—the rocking cots—for those old enough to be out of the cribs so, all in all, our babies and their families do quite well.'

Sophie looked around the big, warm room, not divided off but large enough for each crib to have private space around it. In the far corner a baby was having phototherapy for jaundice, but the light was placed so it shone only on that baby and not onto any of the adjoining cots. She saw two of the little hammocks Albert had mentioned, a little like the baby capsules used in cars, but instead of being fixed they hung from A-frame legs. A swaddled baby lay in each of them, the swing mechanisms so delicate the slightest movement of the baby set them rocking, mimicking the movements the baby would feel if it were still in its mother's womb.

She nodded her approval, remembering how much she'd liked the place on her first visit, and for the first time in hours she felt in control of her life. This was where she belonged...

She wandered around the nursery, looking at the other

babies, most of whom would be gone before she started work next month, seeing the details that had impressed her the first time—tiny flowers and toys embroidered on the stockingette caps the babies wore on their heads, coloured sheets on the specially warmed mattresses in the cribs. These babies were special and the little extra touches proved just how special their carers thought them.

She nodded to other nurses moving quietly around the cribs, and to parents sitting by them, then left the room. She'd collect Thomas, drop Etty home, then go back to the serviced apartment she was renting on a week-to-week basis and ask about renting it for a longer period.

Etty was reading a story to a group of children gathered around her wheelchair, Thomas closest, leaning against one arm of it so his shoulder was touching Etty's knee.

He looked up as Sophie came into the room and his face lit up in a smile so special and familiar she felt her heart turn over. Would she ever get over the miracle of this little boy?

'Aunt Etty's reading a story,' he told her. 'Do I have to go or can we stay until she finishes?'

Aunt Etty already?

'We can stay until she finishes,' Sophie promised Thomas, settling on the floor beside him then, as he sank down onto her knee, putting her arms around him, brushing her cheek against his soft golden curls.

Etty read well, changing voices for the characters—a koala, a kangaroo and a wise old owl—and Sophie smiled to herself, thinking this was kind of like an interview for Etty and wondering if that's what had made her choose to read.

The story finished, Sophie set Thomas on his feet and stood up herself.

'We're going to drive Aunt Etty home,' she said, and Thomas's eyes widened with delighted surprise.

'We are? That's great. Her legs don't work, that's why she has a chair, but she gave some of the kids a ride in the chair. Will she give me a ride if we take her home?'

Etty had wheeled away to put the story book back on a shelf and Sophie didn't answer, thinking it might be better it Thomas didn't get his ride. If he got hooked on Etty, how could Sophie not employ her?

They were back on the riverside drive, Etty having given directions, when a cellphone rang. Etty dug in a pocket of her skirt and answered it, speaking briskly, then doubtfully, saying, 'Well, I'll ask her,' before ending the call.

'That was Gib,' she said, although Sophie had already guessed—guessed too that the question might be about staying to dinner—he was determined to persuade her to take Etty as a carer and probably thought the more time Thomas spent with her, the better.

'He wanted to suggest—'

Etty stopped and Sophie, who'd just turned off the busy road into the quieter street where Gib and Etty lived, glanced towards her. From the little she knew of Etty, not much would faze her.

'You might as well tell me,' she said, pulling into the drive and explaining to Thomas that this was where Etty lived.

'Gib wondered—with the problems you're having finding accommodation—if maybe you'd like to live here.'

Sophie stared at the cottage in front of them, the extensions hidden behind the leafy garden.

'Live here? With him? Why on earth would he think that?'

'Not exactly with him.' Etty hurried to explain. 'The other

wing, the one we've closed off, has a self-contained two-bedroom flat. Gib built it for me when I moved in, but when Gillian died four years ago he was rattling around in his side of it, so I moved over there and we closed the flat. He's often spoken about renting it to someone quiet. You'd be ideal.'

Gillian died?

Had Gillian been his wife?

Four years ago and he still wore her ring?

He must have loved her so much…

Etty was speaking again, something about a kitchen and bathroom and a separate entrance at the side, but even as Sophie pushed away thoughts of Alexander Gibson's wife that were so absolutely none of her business, she knew saying yes to this offer was *not a good idea*!

Confusing though the day had been, this was crystal clear in Sophie's mind. It was one thing to be working for a man who made her feel unsettled, and whose touch sent tremors along her nerves—quite another to be living in close proximity to him.

'It's a wonderful offer but, no, I can't accept it,' Sophie said. Thomas, who hadn't been included in the conversation but had obviously been following at least parts of it, said, 'But if this is Aunt Etty's house then it's got a swimming pool. Aunt Etty was telling us. Couldn't we, please, live here?'

Sophie hardened her heart against the wistful tone, and turned to explain to Thomas that they needed a home of their own. Etty's cellphone rang again, and this time the conversation, on her side at least, was monosyllabic. Two 'nos' and one 'yes' then an 'OK' and that was it.

'Gib said why don't you try it for a month or two—take the flat at least until other housing becomes available? He said once you've lived here for a while and know your way around the city, you'll have a better idea of where you might like to rent.'

'I don't think so,' Sophie began, but Thomas was bouncing in his car seat, yelling, 'Say yes, Sophie, please say yes. Aunt Etty reads the best stories.'

Sophie turned again to study the little boy who'd already lost so much. She saw the blue eyes, so like Hilary's, and the blond curls, the hair colour Hil's though the curls must have been his father's. Resolve melted away. If staying here would make Thomas happy, then who was she to deny him such a simple delight?

'I guess we could stay,' she said, 'but not for ever, you understand. Just until we get a house of our own.'

'With a pool?' he asked, and she nodded.

'With a pool,' she promised him.

Not a good idea! Not a good idea!

She sighed and climbed out of the car, opening the boot, lifting out Etty's wheelchair and setting it by the car door for her, then watching as her son clambered onto the knee of his new best friend and was carried towards the house.

Above them a storm that had threatened all afternoon broke, lightning flashing its vivid warning across the sky, thunder rumbling with a threatening insistence.

Was someone trying to tell her something?

Gib stood beside Andrew Atkins's crib, staring at the little boy, desperate to discover what they were missing. His pager vibrated against his hip, but when he checked the number, it was unfamiliar. A cellphone, but not one he recognised.

Not now, he thought, although he knew if someone had been given his pager number, the call was probably urgent.

He moved out of the unit to make the call from his office down the corridor.

'Sophie Fisher.'

Sophie Fisher paging him? His mind registered surprise while his body—what the hell was his body doing?

Heating?

'It's Gib. You paged me?'

'Yes. I was just thinking. About the little boy—Andrew, wasn't it? I know you've probably checked and that you'd be doing blood and urine values all the time, but I've seen an infant with a very rare but bad reaction to furosemide—I think I saw on the chart that was the diuretic you were using. He was secreting more than twenty times the normal calcium levels and the metabolic imbalances—'

'Sophie, you're a lifesaver—and I think that could be more than a figure of speech. Let me go check. I'll call you back.'

It was late when he called back, but she could hear triumph beneath the exhaustion in his voice.

'I hadn't ever encountered it before, though it's sure to have been written up somewhere,' he said, the shadowy self-blame all doctors shared now overtaking the triumph.

'You've been too close to him,' Sophie reminded him, 'plus trying to do the work of three people, not one.'

'That's no excuse,' he said. 'I should have thought of it.'

'Go home to bed, Gib,' she said softly, and in his head he saw her face—the dark, smoky grey eyes, the straight, thin nose and generous mouth, the black strands of hair framing it—attractive enough...

Until she smiled...

'Gib?'

'Sorry, I was falling asleep on the end of the phone. But before I go, Etty phoned earlier, said you'd agreed to move in. Does that mean you're happy for her to be Thomas's carer—that you'll start work earlier? Help out?'

Silence, then a slow, uncertain 'Yes.'

'That's—'

'But I'll need to talk to you about rosters and duty times. I have something on on Friday week—something I can't put off or not do.'

'I'll organise it,' Gib promised. 'Organise any time off that you need. Having you even a few days a week will be better than going on as we are at the moment. You just tell me when you want to work and I'll take it from there.'

He was so busy being pleased about this outcome it took some time for him to hear the echoes of strain and sadness in her words.

'This something you have to do on Friday week—is it something I can help with?'

A longer pause, and then a strangled, whispered 'No.'

He heard the click as she disconnected and sat looking at his phone for a very long time.

He could have sworn she'd started crying...

CHAPTER THREE

HE'D been at work when they moved in, but returning home on the Saturday evening, he felt the change in the atmosphere of the house—as if it had come to life again. He knew Etty had been spending time with Thomas, first at the child-care centre then going along on shopping expeditions with him and Sophie, picnicking with them one afternoon in the botanical gardens.

He'd felt aggrieved he hadn't been invited, but that had been more because he'd have liked to get to know Sophie better than pursuing his acquaintance with a three-year-old. He was assuring himself it was Sophie as a colleague he wanted to get to know better when Etty called him to dinner.

'Everything OK?' he asked Etty as she bustled around the kitchen, finalising the meal she was preparing for him.

'With Sophie and Thomas? I think so, though I sense Sophie is less delighted than Thomas is with the arrangement. Understandable, living so close to a boss she doesn't really know.'

She paused, and Gib wondered just what was coming next. It wasn't like Etty not to come right out with whatever she needed to say.

'We've got to talk, too,' she finally said, putting down his dinner in front of him. 'About the arrangements here.'

Another pause, then she added, 'I've asked Sophie to come in at nine. I thought with all of us present, we might be able to thrash it out.'

His dinner, a fiery chicken curry that was one of Etty's specialities, suddenly lost taste.

'Thrash what out?'

'My position! I live with you and earn my keep cooking, shopping and housekeeping for you, but if I'm going to work for Sophie, then I should be doing that for her. So I should be paying you board for my room here, and maybe finding someone else to do the housekeeping for you, though if you wanted live-in help, I could shift back into the flat—Sophie says she and Thomas are used to sharing a room and I could have the spare room.'

'But—'

Before Gib could voice his protest there was a soft knock on the door that closed off the second wing from the big living-dining area.

Etty called for Sophie to come in and she entered, dressed in a plain white T-shirt and a white floaty kind of skirt that danced around her ankles as she moved.

'Etty did invite me,' she said hesitantly, while Gib scanned her face for signs of tears, although it had been two days since he'd heard her cry on the telephone.

'You're welcome any time. I know you're officially living in the flat, but feel free to use this room as well.'

She shook her head but half smiled as she said, 'You know not what you're saying! Small boys can reduce a room like this to chaos in five minutes flat. I don't know how they do it, but they seem to trail toys behind them in an invisible cloud, scattering them as they move.'

Sophie reached out and touched the back of a fat leather armchair, needing the support as she tried to settle her nerves. Shifting into this house had been the worst decision she'd ever made, and considering an ill-considered engagement, the purchase of a totally unridable motorbike and a whole wardrobe full of bad garment choices, she'd made some beauties!

The uneasiness she felt when she was with Gib had intensified within his house—even when he wasn't in it—and now, seeing him sitting there, prodding at his dinner while he watched her with an unreadable expression on his face, she felt tension burning through her muscles and stiffening her nerves, so any minute now she'd probably start to shake.

Make a complete idiot of herself!

'Sit.'

Etty gave the order.

'I'll make coffee while Gib finishes his dinner. Take the chair by the window. You'll see the boats that do the dinner cruises going by, and the City Cats—the ferries that run back and forth to the city and beyond. If you've nothing planned for tomorrow, Thomas would love a trip on the ferry. You can take swimming things and get off at Southbank where there's a great beach and swimming area, or take a picnic and go right up to New Farm Park.'

Sophie sat, barely listening to Etty's suggestions but pleased to have something to do that would take her further away from Gib and put her in a position where she wasn't looking directly at him.

'Or you could take Thomas on the ferry, Et,' he said,

making Sophie turn in spite of her unwillingness to look at him. 'And I could take Sophie for an orientation tour of the hospital. I'll probably be too busy to do it on Monday when she starts work, but tomorrow we could do it at our leisure.'

She opened her mouth and then closed it again. It would be good to get a feel for the hospital before she began work—it was just a pity Gib couldn't take Thomas on the ferry and Etty do the hospital bit. She felt safe with Etty.

And not safe with Gib?

Safe? What kind of word was that to be using about people?

'Fine with me,' Etty was saying, and Gib laughed.

'You talk about me bulldozing people, Et,' he said. 'Here we both are, virtually taking over Sophie's life. If you'd like to spend a quiet day at home with Thomas, Sophie, you just say so.'

'I probably should feel put out about it,' she said, smiling at both of them, 'but, in fact, it's quite nice to have someone else telling me what to do. Just lately I've had to make some huge decisions, then sell a house, pack our belongings and organise the move, so having someone making arrangements for me is...' She paused, not wanting them to get the idea she needed—or wanted—that to continue.

'Nice for a change,' Etty finished for her, coming towards her with a tray containing a coffee pot and three cups, and what looked—and smelt—like a freshly baked chocolate cake.

'You've been helping me move in all day—when did you get the time to bake a cake?' Sophie demanded.

Etty smiled at her.

'I'm adept at doing more than one thing at a time,

which is what I wanted to talk to the two of you about. You with us, Gib?'

He stood up and crossed towards them, moving like a man at ease in his skin. And why wouldn't he be? Sophie asked herself, disturbed anew that little things like the way he moved should be on her mind.

'I thought perhaps the two of you could share me,' Etty began. 'I can stay where I am on Gib's side of the house, with a baby monitor connecting me to Thomas's room when Sophie's on duty or on call at night, take care of Thomas during the day when he's not at child care, even drop him there or collect him from there when it suits you, Sophie. But if you're at home, I'll keep out of the way so you have your special time with him. If you're at home, you do his bath and dinner and the putting-to-bed routine, while I do dinner out here, then when he's settled, is there any reason why you can't have your dinner with Gib and me—or just with me if Gib's not here?'

Etty hesitated but Sophie's mind had stalled at the prospect of dining with her boss every night and she couldn't find the words to protest.

'Of course,' Etty continued, as if their silence had been acceptance of the plan thus far, 'if you're working late, Sophie, Thomas will be my first concern. I can still feed Gib when Thomas has gone to bed or, if necessary, Gib can fend for himself. He's not bad in the kitchen.'

Sophie finally caught up with the conversation.

'I don't need to eat with you two every night. I'm quite happy with my own company.'

'I doubt there'll be many meals we share,' Gib told her, 'given the situation at the hospital. If I'm not on duty or on call, then you will be, but I can understand you'd want some privacy, so can we leave it that if you're at home Etty will prepare your dinner? And you're very welcome to eat with us should you wish to, but we certainly won't be offended if you don't.'

He doesn't want this false intimacy any more than I do, Sophie realised, then told herself the little squirm of disquiet she felt couldn't possibly be disappointment. Right now she had to sort out her own and Thomas's lives, not get involved with a man. Particularly not a man who still lived with the memory of his dead wife!

Etty poured two cups of coffee, passed them and the chocolate cake around, then excused herself to make some phone calls. Sophie sipped her coffee and tasted the cake— delicious—staring out the wide windows to the river and feeling unaccountably relaxed.

'I usually go up to the hospital at eight on Sunday mornings,' Gib said, the words quietly spoken so they barely ruffled the peaceful tenor of the room. 'Is that too early for you?'

Sophie turned towards him with a smile.

'Apparently you've never lived with a three-year-old. Thomas's day begins with the dawn chorus of the magpies and the cackling laughter of the kookaburras.'

'So you never get to sleep in?' He was leaning back in the armchair, his feet propped on the footstool, and his smile was as slow and relaxed as his attitude.

But neither word came near to describing Sophie's reaction to that smile—a reaction that ran swiftly along her skin and tightened the nerves beneath it, while her stomach quivered with an uncertain delight.

Oh, dear!

'I don't mind not sleeping in,' she managed to say, mentally whacking herself on the side of her head for her stupidity in putting herself in this position—not to mention the stupidity of being attracted to her boss. Was it because it had been so long since she'd been attracted to anyone that this was happening? So long since she'd had time to think about men in a man-woman attraction kind of way?

'Good, then we'll leave at eight, shall we? We can go in my car. Yui's on duty so I'll just check the unit then show you around the hospital—introduce you to the weekend staff and let you get a feel for the place.'

'And little Andrew, how is he?'

Safe question. Work talk was good. Maybe if they could keep it up, moving in wouldn't be quite the disaster she'd been picturing.

'We swapped him to a different diuretic. With the fluid in his lungs we didn't want to take him off it altogether. He's picked up amazingly in just one day. Was it ever written up, the case you knew of where there'd been a bad reaction?'

'I...'

She stopped, remembering the other case and when it had occurred—remembering Hil, six months pregnant, coming home with the news that she had breast cancer.

'My boss asked me to do it, but...'

Keep talking, she told herself, but she couldn't. Her chest was tight, her throat closed up by a lump as big as Brisbane. Heaven help her! Why was this happening now? She'd been so good—so together—so why now, in front of her new boss, was she falling apart? Damn it all, she could feel tears leaking from the corners of her eyes. She lifted her hands and used the tips of her fingers to wipe them away, heart pounding as she tried to breathe normally.

Gib watched the long, slim fingers with their pale, pared-down nails brush against her cheeks. He knew she was wiping tears away and knew as well she'd hate it if he mentioned it. Yet every instinct said to go to her, to offer comfort.

'I didn't get it done,' she said eventually, while he remained rooted in his armchair, denying instinct, wondering what was happening to him that his chest should feel so tight. 'Stuff was happening in my life back then. I should have done it because it might have saved Andrew suffering discomfort, not to mention his parents and the staff going into a panic over his condition. It might have saved all the other Andrews as well.'

Stuff had been happening in her life? Fairly traumatic stuff from the tears. He wanted, quite unreasonably, to know what it had been—to know a lot more about this woman who had come into his life.

But he could hardly ask…

'Your boss must have known you hadn't done it. He could have written it up himself, or had someone else do it. That was his job!'

She was OK now, straightening at the rebuke he couldn't keep out of his voice, but the rebuke wasn't aimed at her but at the man or woman who hadn't followed through on the writing of the paper.

'I guess he had other things on his mind,' she said quietly, then she switched the conversation to protocols they followed with pre-term births.

Not a good conversational change as Gib was reminded of a baby he'd lost earlier this week.

'We've a resus area set aside in one of the delivery suites and like to have a full team on hand when a baby is born pre-term or with an expected low birth weight. Less than thirty weeks or smaller than one kilogram, we intubate as a matter of course. We do external heart massage, using the chest-encircling technique for bradycardia, use epinephrine and atropine if necessary, generally manage hypotension with whole blood—all the usual things, but the big thing as far as we're concerned is stabilising the infant before he or she leaves the delivery suite.'

'I think the figures on neonates that have to be moved to special units before they get expert help prove just how beneficial immediate resuscitation is,' she said, 'and it's great that all new maternity wards in hospitals with NICUs have facilities for us to work within the delivery suite. The old delivery rooms were so cramped it was nearly impossible.'

Which led to talk of where she'd worked, both in Australia and for a short time overseas, but though she spoke easily and even smiled at him occasionally, the image of those long fingers, surreptitiously wiping tears off her smooth cheeks, stayed in his head.

Thomas was swimming in the pool with Etty when they left for the hospital the next morning, Etty furnished with a list of his likes and dislikes, and orders to insist that Thomas wear his hat outside, no matter how much he objected.

'You're uneasy. Have you not left him with a sitter before?' Gib asked, as they drove towards the hospital.

'More uneasy for Etty. He's exhausting.'

'Knowing Etty, she'll have him organised in no time. She'd have loved for us—'

He stopped so abruptly Sophie glanced towards him, seeing the rather stern profile—high forehead, straight nose and stubborn chin—and the dark hair with silver streaks, curling into his neck where it still needed a cut.

He turned as if her scrutiny had touched him and she

saw dark blue eyes that held shadows of sadness too deep to measure.

'Etty told me your wife died,' Sophie said carefully. 'Was she ill or was it an accident?'

He didn't answer, and Sophie wondered if she'd crossed some invisible boundary he'd prefer to keep erected between them. Then, just as she was about to introduce a safe work topic, he spoke.

'She was driving up the north coast highway—hit a semi-trailer. I'd like to think it was an accident,' he said, so gravely Sophie felt a chill run through her body. 'But unfortunately for my peace of mind, I think it more likely she took her own life. She had a form of manic depression—bipolar—controlled to a certain extent by drugs—when she took them.'

The last phrase had been added under his breath and Sophie suspected she hadn't been meant to hear it, but the pain in his voice throughout his explanation was the same pain she'd seen in his eyes. He must have loved her very much. Gillian, her name was—Etty had mentioned it...

He turned the car into the hospital grounds then wound up and up on a multi-level car park.

'There's a parking space for you here,' he said, as if their conversation had never strayed from work-related matters. 'See, your name's already painted on the board.'

It was indeed, but Sophie's thoughts hadn't shifted quite as easily as his—or as he was pretending his had. She was still thinking of a woman in so much mental pain that driving her car into a semi-trailer had seemed the only way to relieve it.

'The exit over there brings us straight onto the NICU floor, and the rooms where we see follow-up patients are here as well.'

He led the way into an unfamiliar corridor.

'Offices down this side—here's the one you'll have, although we haven't liked to clean Pete's stuff out of it. I'll speak to him then get Marilyn onto it tomorrow. The next room is a general doctors' room—consultants use it if they want somewhere to work while they're here. On the other side, we have our own path lab and a small procedures room.'

'I was reading about your neonatal cardiac surgical team—they have a separate unit?'

Gib nodded, opening a door and showing her into a brightly decorated waiting room.

'On the same floor but in the wing on the other side of the lift foyer. This is our suite—the waiting room, reception area, two consulting rooms and file room. We've a secretary, nurse and Marilyn, the receptionist. She's the one who rules our lives, making sure we're where we're supposed to be and when. The secretaries come and go— they roster through the hospital secretarial pool—but Marilyn has been here since before I began work at the hospital and as that was as an intern, it's a long time ago.'

'How old are you?'

Had she really asked that? The astonished look on Gib's face matched her own disbelief that such a personal question had slipped out.

'I'm sorry, that's absolutely none of my business,' she managed, but he'd stopped looking astonished now and was almost smiling.

'But I know how old you are. It was on your job application. So why shouldn't you know my age?'

Sophie was thankful she wasn't given to blushing. She was so hot with embarrassment she'd be tomato red all over.

'I don't need to— It was stupid— I was thinking—'

'I'm forty-two,' he said gravely, although the smile still lingered about his lips, visible also in the little crinkly lines at the corners of his eyes. 'Does that make me an old man in your eyes?'

A teasing question—nothing more—yet to Sophie there seemed to be a subtext she didn't understand, as if he might not want her thinking him old.

Or was she adding subtexts because of the way he affected her?

'Hardly in your dotage,' she assured him. 'Though I noticed the pharmacy on the ground floor had a good range in walking sticks.'

'Cheeky minx!' he said, cuffing her lightly on the shoulder as they moved on down the corridor.

He's a nice man. The thought startled Sophie almost as much as her question had earlier. But he was, and so she smiled at him.

Gib knew he should smile back, but his wedding ring was growing tight around his finger and his practical self was demanding to know how he'd got himself into this fix. Not only was he going to be working with this woman who looked so beautiful when she smiled, but she was living in his house! How had that happened?

Because it had been so long since he'd felt attraction for a woman, he'd decided he was over it—that it had stopped happening for him.

'Shall we continue our tour?'

He must have been staring at her, for the smile had gone, replaced by a look of trepidation, and the question, when she'd asked it, had sounded forced.

'I guess we should.'

He held the door for her then led her further down the

corridor, pointing out the various types of equipment they had on hand.

The final room was a wash room, where they stood at adjoining sinks and scrubbed their hands and arms, before gowning up and stringing masks around their necks in case they were needed. Gib handed Sophie a couple of pairs of gloves, shoving some for himself into the pocket of his gown.

'The unit was originally planned for six babies at a time, but was expanded to ten when we modernised it. At the moment we have nine. You've met Andrew, and the others are doing well, with the exception of little Mackenzie Kennedy. We picked up on possible NEC when her mother mentioned something about how well she was doing, and pointed to her fat little tummy.'

Necrotising enterocolitis—Sophie thought about the insidious disease as she followed Gib to the sick baby's crib.

'Has she had to have part of her intestine removed?' Sophie asked him, knowing that if only the inner lining of the bowel was affected it could regrow, but if a whole section of the bowel died it would have to be surgically cut out and the two healthy pieces joined together in a later operation.

'Not yet. She's really too fragile for surgery so we immediately went NPO—we use the Latin *nil per os* initials instead of nil by mouth in the unit—and now have her on IV nutrition and we're suctioning her stomach to remove air and fluid.'

He paused by a crib, set, as they all were, a good distance from the nearest one. Beside it sat a pale woman, her hand through the port in the crib wall, one finger poked into the baby's unresponsive hand.

Gib introduced Maria Kennedy, who nodded at Sophie in that semi-somnolent way exhausted parents often had.

Sophie leant over the crib, seeing the tiny child spread-eagled on the warm mattress, tubes and monitors almost obscuring the fact this was a tiny human being. Then she looked up at Maria.

'Does she react well to touch?'

Maria looked surprised, as if doctors didn't normally ask her that kind of question, but Sophie knew preemies were often stressed by touch, and had to grow used to it.

'She seems to know I'm here if I put my hand near hers,' Maria said, and although she spoke very quietly, Mackenzie's translucent eyelids opened and blue eyes stared vacantly upwards.

'Here, little girl,' Maria said softly, and the baby's eyes tracked slightly in her direction.

'Well done,' Sophie said, then realised she shouldn't have sounded so chirpy for Maria was crying, tears streaming down her cheeks, a handkerchief pressed to her lips as she tried to muffle her sobs.

A nurse was moving towards them, but Sophie was faster, putting her arm around the distressed woman's shoulders and helping her out of her chair.

'A room we can use?' she murmured at Gib above Maria's head.

'This way,' he said, and led them out, past the nurse and the other cribs, parents turning to watch their little procession.

The quiet room was furnished with soft armchairs and a sofa, while against one wall a table held a steaming urn, cups and saucers, coffee and tea bags, and tins of cake and biscuits.

Sophie urged Maria towards the sofa, then held the woman while she cried, waiting until the sobs subsided before offering a tissue from a box on the table beside the sofa.

How many boxes of tissues a year would be needed in

this room where parents with breaking hearts tried to come to terms with their new baby's fragility?

'Are you concerned that she's sick?' Gib asked, when Maria eventually lifted her head from Sophie's shoulder and stared blankly around the room.

A minuscule movement of the head—definitely negative.

'Why don't we all grab a cup of tea or coffee?' Sophie suggested. 'You might feel able to talk about things when you've had something to eat and drink.'

Another barely noticeable movement, but this time more nod than shake.

'Tea?' Sophie pursued, and now Maria smiled. It wasn't much of a smile, but at least it showed her self-control was returning.

'Coffee, two sugars,' she said, but when Sophie moved to stand up and get it, Gib held up his hand.

'Allow me. What will you have, Sophie?'

'Coffee, please, no sugar, no milk.'

'All you doctors live on coffee—I never understood why until this happened.'

Maria's voice broke on the last word, and Sophie reached out to hold her again.

'You're doing fine,' she said. 'Heaven knows, it must be hard enough to have a new healthy baby to care for, but having one who needs so much extra attention, it would scare the living daylights out of me.'

'It's all right while she's in here,' Maria said, turning fear-filled eyes towards Sophie. 'Here there are monitors and tubes and nurses and doctors, but what happens when I get her home and something like this—this gut thing she's got—happens there?'

'We'll still be here for you,' Gib assured her. 'Any time,

day or night, you can phone the number we'll give you and a doctor or nurse that you know from the unit will be there to answer your questions or give you advice. If you're really worried, you bring her straight back to the hospital and one of us will see her down in Emergency. She's our baby too now. Part of our family.'

Maria smiled at him but Sophie could feel the woman trembling and knew they hadn't reached the crux of her concern. She thanked Gib for the coffee he set on the table in front of them and waited until Maria had sipped at hers before asking, 'You do know we'll keep Mackenzie here until her intestines are behaving properly and she's feeding well, and breathing on her own. We wouldn't send her home while she needs special help and expect you to cope with that alone.'

'It's not that part,' Maria said. 'I know you'll get her right, but it's me—what if I can't do things right for her at home? The nurse tells me how to wrap her and how to lay her on her side so her legs curl up, but what if I get that part wrong? Or I have too much light or too much noise?'

She began to cry again.

'It's already my fault that she's early, so what if I make things worse for her at home instead of better? Then it will be my fault again that she's not catching up with other babies her age.'

'Oh!' Sophie said, looking up at Gib, wondering if he wanted her to answer or if he, knowing the woman and the circumstances of the birth, would step in.

He gave a shrug but the angry frown on his face suggested he was about to find whoever it was who'd overloaded poor Maria with information and string him or her up by the thumbs.

'Maria,' Sophie began, turning to face the distraught woman and taking hold of her free hand. 'I don't know Mackenzie's history but unless you were jumping out of a plane without a parachute before you had her, I doubt very much if her premature birth was your fault. We all tend to blame ourselves when things go wrong, but it's just bad luck and we have to accept that then see what we can do to make things better.'

She waited while Maria drank more coffee.

'You're already doing that—I saw Mackenzie, sick though she is right now, turn towards your voice. A lot of babies in the NICU never manage that much recognition of their parents' voices. And as for looking after her at home, do you love her?'

Maria nodded, and smiled through her tears.

'From the moment I knew I was pregnant I loved her. I talked to her and sang her songs and played with her with my hand on my tummy when she kicked.'

'That's probably why she recognises your voice. And will always do so. Here, in an NICU, we do all the medical and physical things we can to give the babies in our care the best possible start we can, but only you, a parent, can give them love. We can tell you to hold them this way, and to try to get them into good sleep patterns, and to swaddle them so their little legs tuck up, but the main thing every baby needs is love. As long as Mackenzie hears your love for her in your voice, and feels it in your touch, she'll be fine. As Gib said, the staff are here for you as back-up with all the other stuff, and although when people hand you reams of information about caring for your preemie and it's impossible to absorb when all you're worried about is whether she will live or die, you'll soon get the hang of things, mainly because she'll tell you.'

Was she talking too much? Sophie glanced at Gib, who was leaning back against the table, his arms crossed across his chest, his body language suggesting he'd be happy for her to keep talking all day.

'Tell me?' Maria repeated, and Sophie smiled at her.

'Of course she will. You probably already know when she's upset. Think about what happens when you or one of the staff handle her—what does she like? What doesn't she like?'

'She doesn't like to be held in one hand.'

Sophie chuckled at the positive response. She knew exactly what Maria meant, having occasionally seen a staff member display a tiny baby in one hand, usually marvelling that he or she could be held that way.

'And how do you know that?' she asked Maria.

'She gets pink, like she's angry, and it seems to me she has to breathe faster.'

'There you are. She's already telling you things—and you're reading her beautifully. I'm not saying you'll always do things exactly right, or that sometimes—maybe often— you won't feel angry and frustrated because you *don't* know what's wrong with her, but you'll be learning all the time, and she'll get better and better at her communication. Eventually, of course, as her lungs develop and she's better able to know something's wrong with her, she'll start fretting and crying when she's uncomfortable, and you'll get the message loud and clear.'

'Then I'll probably end up giving in to her and spoil her,' Maria said, but the tears were gone and she was smiling at Sophie.

'My gran always said you can't spoil babies,' Sophie told her, patting the hand she was holding and then releasing it.

Maria stood up, saying she had to get back to Mackenzie, but as Sophie made to follow her, Gib put out his hand and touched her arm, stopping her in mid-stride. She looked at him, wondering what he wanted, waiting for him to speak—too close to him to feel comfortable…

'I— That shocked me, Maria worrying like that over taking Mackenzie home. Here I've been sailing along, thinking how good and clever we are to have covered every possible contingency we can think of and giving parents all the information we possible can, and what we're, in fact, doing is terrifying them. Taking their baby home should be a special, joyous thing, not cause for even more anxiety.'

Sophie stepped back, needing to put space between herself and Gib, pleased she had work to talk about so she didn't have to think about her body's reaction to that casual, meaningless touch—to his closeness.

'Don't get all hung up about it,' she told him. 'Maria found the information overwhelming, but someone else might have wanted more. You can't gauge how much every individual parent can absorb, so all you can do is have the information available, explain what you can, answer questions when they're asked, and, as you do, have a help-line available for the questions no one thought of when the information booklets were prepared.'

'Like how do you stop hiccups? That was the first question I was asked when I was the bunny on the help-line during my early neonatal training. I didn't have a clue, and was considering all kinds of tricks I'd tried myself—could a mother breast-feed upside down?—when a kindly sister told me no one had a clue and usually they just went away.'

Sophie smiled at the story but, rather than smiling back at her, Gib frowned.

'Come on,' he said. 'We're here to tour the hospital and so far you've only seen the one part of it, you know.'

He led the way out of the quiet room but not back into the NICU. Sophie followed, uncertain what had happened to change him from a joking colleague to a boss again.

Not that it wasn't for the best. She might be attracted to the man but she had no intention of falling in love with someone who still wore his wedding ring four years after his wife's death.

Had Sunday's guided tour helped her settle in, or was Sophie Fisher simply the most efficient colleague he'd ever encountered?

Gib was pondering the question as he sat in his office late on Wednesday afternoon. He was through work for the day, mainly because his new consultant had taken half his follow-up patients and a number of their parents had left messages with Marilyn so he knew none of them had objected to not seeing him in person.

She—Sophie not Marilyn—had made the suggestion she take some of them late that morning, when, by some miracle he was reasonably sure wasn't entirely to do with his new team member, all their babies—apart from Mackenzie who was still on parenteral feeds, but appeared to be stabilising—were resting quietly—thriving even—not one of them showing imminent signs of NEC, or RDS, or BPD, or any of the other alphabet soup of complications neonates could suffer.

'It would be nice to see some of your follow-up cases,' was how she'd phrased it, and he'd been about to suggest she sit in on his consultations when Marilyn got involved, calmly decreeing which clients Sophie should take and which should go to him.

He was considering whether Sophie would become another female organiser in his life, joining Etty and Marilyn in their roles, when she knocked briskly on his door then toed it open, coming in with an armload of files.

'Marilyn was saying that not all the old files have been computerised,' she said, sitting down in one of his visitor chairs and resting the files in her lap. 'I thought, if you didn't mind, I could start doing some of them.'

'Computerising them? Why would you want to do that? There are dozens of people already employed in this hospital whose job it is to do it, so I assume it will all eventually get done. And when would you have time? I know we've finished early today but, believe me, that's an exception rather than the rule.'

She smiled at him, and though he was now used to the way this expression transformed her face, something inside him still stirred when he saw it. Though it wasn't only the smile—something inside him stirred when he just thought of her, something he hadn't felt for so long he was uncertain about its origins!

Well! Not entirely uncertain…

'I won't do them all at once, and as for time, take tonight, and tomorrow night. I'm on duty so I'll be here at the hospital and I'll be bored to tears if there are no crises. Then consider that if I'm going to be seeing follow-up clients when they come for appointments, I need to know their histories. But why just read the files when I can be typing them into a computer at the same time? I know the system they use here—my part-time job as a student was entering hospital files into computer systems.'

He stared at her, then shook his head, unable to believe she could be giving herself so much extra work.

'Are you sure you *want* to do this?'

Another smile. 'As against Marilyn beating me with her feather duster and insisting I get cracking on it?' she teased, and Gib knew it was more than her smile he found attractive.

Why her?

Why now?

Did it matter?

There'd been other women since Gillian had died. Women he'd dated for a while, enjoying their company, but always making sure they knew it was only for a while— that a serious, long-term relationship wasn't and never would be on the cards.

How could it be when he'd already failed one woman so badly?

And Sophie, a single parent with responsibilities to her little boy, wouldn't be a candidate for a short-term affair. If, indeed, she wanted a relationship of any kind!

He had no idea.

'Can I take your silence as a yes?' she said, still smiling slightly, or maybe not smiling, although a teasing note was lilting through the words.

'Of course,' he managed, wondering how long he'd sat there, contemplating things that had nothing whatsoever to do with computerising patient files.

Cautiously balancing her armload, she stood up, smiled again and walked towards the door. Gib's eyes were on her slim, straight back and the neat roll of black hair—his mind wondering what it looked like down, splayed across her pale skin…

Or a pillow…

CHAPTER FOUR

THURSDAY began badly and got worse. At two in the morning, the sister on duty called Sophie to say Mackenzie's condition was deteriorating.

They'd been worried about her all week, as she was losing weight in spite of the IV feeding, but when Sophie had checked her at 10 p.m. before heading to the on-duty room for a sleep, she had been stable.

'Temp up, rapid heart rate—the little mite is really battling.' The look of strain on Albert's face told her how stressed he was over this special charge.

Abdominal X-rays, now being taken every six hours, had shown Mackenzie had progressed to stage two of the disease. When her 6 p.m. blood test revealed a drop in platelets to below twenty thousand, Sophie had infused replacement platelets, staying in the unit until test results showed the increase.

Now she had to worry if the infusion had somehow caused the deterioration in Mackenzie's condition or if something else had happened. She checked everything, knowing the little girl needed more fluids and electrolytes than other babies her size because of the fluid loss from her intestines.

'Perforated bowel?'

Albert whispered the words Sophie didn't want to hear. Mackenzie was far too small for an operation to remove damaged bowel, but if liquid from her gut was leaking into her abdomen it would be poisoning her whole system in spite of the antibiotics they were pumping into her.

'Let's take another X-ray, and see what we can see,' Sophie said. Albert needed no second telling, removing monitor leads before moving the baby, crib and all, to the imaging room.

The X-ray results showed the symptoms of NEC but it was hard to see a perforation.

'I'll put a drain into her abdomen, and we'll test what we get out of it for any strains of bacteria we might not be treating. Maybe changing the antibiotics will help until Gib and the surgeons decide if she needs a laparotomy.'

They shifted Mackenzie to the procedures room, where Sophie inserted a small tube to drain fluid from the little girl's abdomen. She ordered increased suctioning of her stomach, warning Albert at the same time of the need for care so the fragile, immature cells lining the stomach and intestines didn't suffer further damage.

Then they waited, knowing with tiny neonates they should see a quick response if the measures they had taken were going to work.

'Looking good,' Albert said at last, and Sophie had to agree. The little girl had stabilised, but this was only a temporary measure. If her bowel was perforated and continued to leak its contents into the abdomen, surgery would be the only option, no matter how small she was.

As Sophie made her way back to the on-duty room, thinking a couple of hours' sleep would be better than none, she wondered if she'd done the right thing, taking the decision to insert the drain. Should she have called Gib?

Gib. Amazing how easy it was to call him that now. And amazing how helpful and supportive he'd been throughout the week, guiding her into their way of doing things without preaching or taking over himself.

Gentle with the patients and with their parents—care and compassion in everything he did.

Nice man.

Thoroughly nice man!

Thoroughly nice man who made her feel things she didn't want to feel…

'So, little Mackenzie, what are we going to do with you?'

They were doing rounds and although Sophie had seen Gib earlier and told him about the drama in the wee hours of the morning, he hadn't made any comment, content to let her complete her account of all that had happened. But there were two men she hadn't met before at rounds, one introduced as a paediatric surgeon, the other as a gastro-enterologist. Both here for Mackenzie, she assumed, which was why this particular baby had been left until last.

'Perhaps Dr Fisher will tell us where we are at with Mackenzie,' Gib said, and it took Sophie a minute to remember she was Dr Fisher, as first names were the norm in this NICU.

Sophie ran through the events leading up to their suspicions of NEC.

'She'd been on enteral feeding for four days, with very small increases in volume each day. She then showed typical symptoms—less active, more incidents of apnoea, respiratory problems, vomiting and greenish stools. But it was the mother who pointed out her slightly distended tummy. We shifted her to NPO and began parenteral feeding. Her condition improved, and we were considering trying her again on enteral feeding when she showed signs of severe sepsis at two this morning. X-rays showed mucosal necrosis and submucosal haemorrhage with some intramural air pockets. I inserted an abdomen drain and, after a culture of a fluid sample from the drain, changed her antibiotics.'

'Was the X-ray clear enough to see a perforation?' The gastroenterologist asked the question.

'No,' Sophie told him. 'There were dark areas that could have been damaged bowel or blood. There was no way to tell, although the scans Dr Gibson ordered when he came on duty this morning might show what's happening more clearly. I haven't seen those yet.'

'They don't,' Gib said. 'I had our top imaging techs at work, but there's no way you can sort out what's happening in that tiny abdomen.'

'She'll need a laparotomy?' the surgeon asked, and Sophie knew from something in his voice that he would find the challenge of operating on so small a child quite exciting.

'Hard to agree to when she's so small, but if we don't do it we'll never know what's going on in there,' Gib told him.

'And is that all you want—find out what's going on?' the gastroenterologist asked.

Million-dollar question! In a larger and more stable child, if a piece of dead bowel was found, it could be resected—cut out—and the two healthy ends joined. If the damage was severe, then the upper end could be diverted out through the skin in a stoma then later, in a second operation, joined up again. But intestines could also heal themselves, as the gastroenterologist was subtly reminding the gathering.

So who would make the decision? Sophie wondered as the surgeon and gastroenterologist argued amiably, mainly for the benefit of the interns and medical students attending the rounds. Mackenzie's parents would be consulted and would have the final say on any major procedure the doctors would perform on Mackenzie, but would Gib just listen to both the consultants and weigh things up himself before he put it to the parents, or did he favour taking the advice of the specialists he called in?

Sophie didn't have to wait long to find out.

'I know she's small, but I think the operation is the only way we'll find out what is happening,' Gib said. 'But we need to talk about the risks involved so I can explain them to the parents. Sophie, come with us—we'll put together some figures for mortality and morbidity rates in operations in case Maria and Josh ask.'

'But surely the mortality rate for not operating if the bowel is perforated is one hundred per cent,' the surgeon said, as Sophie followed the other three specialists towards Gib's office. 'Isn't that the only stat they'll need to know?'

'Not really,' Sophie said quietly, when they were all seated. 'They'll want to know how the operation will affect Mackenzie, not only now but in the future. They'll want to know if it's worth putting her through this operation when she's already so frail and sick. Will it make her better? Can we tell them that? Not really. All we can say is that it might. I don't know that giving already stressed parents percentages is much help. What are the figures? Off the top of my head, something like forty-seven per cent are OK after surgery, but that's with older, larger and definitely more stable infants. Even with all the odds in their favour, ten per cent have significant gastro-intestinal problems for ever and fifteen per cent end up with damage to their central nervous system—and that's not counting the ones that have other negative conse-quences of the operation.'

'Are you saying don't tell them?' the surgeon demanded. 'We've a duty of care, a duty to disclose these things.'

'I know,' Sophie said, suddenly feeling so tired she was sorry she'd started arguing. 'But they hear the forty-seven per cent and think, wow, that's nearly half, but no one's done studies of ops on babies as immature as Mackenzie. The positive result percentage could be as low as ten for all we know.'

'Or less than ten,' Gib put in, 'but do we have an alter-native?'

'Only palliative care,' Sophie said.

'That's another way of saying let her die,' the surgeon snapped, and Sophie took a deep breath to stop herself snapping right back.

'Not necessarily. We can continue to treat her for the in-fection, monitor her more closely and hopefully build her up to the stage where she's strong enough that her chances of surviving an operation are considerably increased.'

'Gib, this is your decision,' the surgeon said, although the gastroenterologist had shown a hint of support for Sophie with a nod of his head in her direction.

'I'll talk to her parents and let you know,' Gib replied.

'Today?' the surgeon persisted, but Gib remained calm.

'If possible, but you know how it is. They'll need time to think about it and probably discuss it with family members or their own GP, perhaps a religious advisor if they have a particular faith. I won't push them into a decision they might afterwards regret.'

'And if she dies while they're deciding?'

'Would that be worse than her dying on the operating table after they've agreed to go ahead?' Sophie demanded, angry that the man kept pushing Gib, angry that Maria and Josh would have to make this terrible decision.

She was a fighter, not a quitter, Gib realised as she faced down the surgeon with those stormy grey eyes. They needed fighters in a neonatal unit—babies who were fighters, parents who were fighters and staff who would stand up to anyone if they thought it was in the best interests of their charges.

But he was still the team leader and he had to make the decision—operate now or wait.

'What will you do?' Sophie asked when the two consultants had left the room.

Gib smiled at her.

'Surely it will be the parents' decision,' he teased, and she gave a huff of derision.

'As if!' she muttered, apparently still angry from the surgeon's words. 'The poor parents listen to what we tell them, and pretend to think about it—no, that's not fair, of course they think about it—but they don't really understand and as far as they're concerned the doctor—i.e. you—is God, and in the end they will inevitably ask you what you recommend. And they'll go along with whatever it is—that's the decision they'll make!'

'True enough,' he said. Hearing it put like that made him feel depressed, although he knew the weight of these decisions he had to make was a personal burden he was fated to carry for ever.

Would it help to share it?

He'd never had a neonatologist on his team with as much experience as Sophie had. Perhaps sharing it might be an idea.

'You had plenty to say before—do you really believe we should wait?'

She raised her head and studied his face, her eyes scanning across it as if she hadn't seen it before—or perhaps trying to read behind it and discover the consequences of her answering his question.

'I think she'd be too unstable for an op today,' she said, then frowned. 'No, that's wrong. I think she's too unstable for an op this morning, but the situation can change so quickly with these infants that this afternoon it might be different.'

'And if it came to operate or lose her?'

'Oh, Gib,' she said, so softly his name came across the desk like the whisper of a lover. 'I really, really hate those decisions, but I know they have to be made. I'd say operate, of course I would, but with Mackenzie, I feel she's picked up enough since 2 a.m. for the decision not to be critical—not to be immediate.'

'The neonatal cardiac team operate on babies far more fragile than Mackenzie,' Gib said, enjoying playing devil's advocate with this woman whose work he was learning to respect.

'It's operate or lose them,' Sophie reminded him, then she smiled as she added, 'And I've already given you my answer to that situation.'

Her face wasn't exactly ordinary without the smile, so why did the smile make such a difference?

'Do you want me with you when you talk to them?'

He shook off the distraction of Sophie's smile and agreed he'd like her presence.

'You've already established a rapport with Maria and,

though Josh is a forceful presence, I think behind the scenes it's Maria who's the boss. Say an hour?'

Sophie nodded and left the room, anxious to check Mackenzie again, although it wasn't long since she'd seen her. With rounds finished, Maria and Josh were both with their baby, the tall, solid rugby player making Mackenzie seem even tinier.

'What's happening?' Maria asked, and Sophie realised she should have kept away until she and Gib could approach them together.

'She's stabilised a lot since last night,' she answered, then she checked the monitors and excused herself, feeling bad because the information she had to put together was going to increase the load of strain these already stressed parents carried.

'Let's lunch,' Gib said to Sophie, as they left the family room where they'd laid out all the pros and cons of operating on a baby as small as Mackenzie and given the parents the details of the operation she might need. He guided Sophie back into his office, stopping just inside the door to issue what might have been an invitation.

She felt exhausted, not from lack of sleep but from the emotional tension of their conversation with Josh and Maria.

'I was going to go down to the child-care centre and play with Thomas for a short time. Last night was the first stint of on-duty work I've done and I really missed him.'

'Etty's very good,' Gib said, frowning at her as though somehow she'd maligned his aunt-in-law.

'I have no doubt she is, but it's not Thomas I was worried about—it's me. After what we've just been through, I need a hug.'

'I can do hugs,' he said quietly, and Sophie felt all the blood stop running in her veins as a stillness she didn't want to break fell between them. Then she saw his hand rise towards her—his left hand with the wedding ring.

'Maybe not,' she said, then was disappointed when he echoed her.

'Maybe not.'

Two words—whispered almost—sliding into her ears with a strange resonance as if they weren't a denial but a promise.

'But come to lunch with me before you visit Thomas for your hug. You've been up half the night and are on duty again tonight, so take an hour or two off this afternoon— for Thomas's hugs.'

Lunch sounded good and although lunching with Gib— spending any more time than absolutely necessary with Gib—wasn't a particularly good idea, given how 'nice' she was beginning to find him, it would be good to discuss Mackenzie, and the other babies in their care, in less clinical surroundings.

'Have you tried the café off the foyer?'

Gib had taken her acquiescence for granted and was guiding her towards the lift.

'I haven't tried anything but the sandwiches in the staffroom fridge,' she told him, feeling the skin-alert his closeness usually caused and wondering if familiarity might breed not contempt, in this case, but some kind of immunity from her physical responses to this man's presence.

'Then you're in for a treat. Angelique, who runs the café, is a chef in her own right, and employs the best young apprentices from the local colleges.'

The lift stopped on the ground floor, and once again he stepped close, guiding her with his hand to her elbow, a courtly gesture—old-fashioned in its politeness—but as potent as a kiss to Sophie's skin.

Seated opposite her at one of the small tables in the café, Gib wondered why he'd asked her.

To talk work, of course.

But was it?

Wasn't it more the effect of the smile?

She was studying the menu, a slight frown creasing the smooth skin of her brow. Her hair was pulled back into its usually neat pleat, the way she'd worn it for the interview and always wore it to work, but he'd seen it falling from a loose knot when she played with Thomas on the terrace below the house and—

'Pizza with chicken, banana, bacon, tomato and chilli sauce?' She glanced up at him across the menu, grey eyes smiling, although he couldn't see her lips.

'It's great,' he told her, 'and if you're only having a slice or two, try the watermelon salad with it.'

'Sounds perfect,' she said, setting down the menu so he could see her whole face, smile and all. 'And a lemon squash, I think. That way I get...' she counted on her long, slim fingers '...four of my fruit and veg out of the way for the day. Is it nine we're supposed to have?'

How could she be so at ease when he was as tense as a tightened guitar string whenever he was near her? She'd been in his life less a week, and already he was more distracted than he'd been since—since when? Gillian's diagnosis? The first time she'd been hospitalised? Her death?

Over the last four years he'd learned to think less and less about Gillian, but since meeting Sophie—

'The waitress wondered if you're ready to order.'

Sophie's gentle words broke into his reverie and he

looked up to see the young woman standing by his chair, pencil poised over her notebook.

'I'll have what she's having,' he said, then, hearing Sophie's laughter, realised it was a well-worn phrase that had originated in an old movie. Then he remembered the circumstances in which it had been said and felt distinctly uncomfortable!

Sophie was still smiling as she handed her menu to the waitress, but as silence stretched between them she rearranged her place setting to hide the unsettled feeling the chance remark had caused. Although now the meal had been ordered they could talk about Mackenzie, for surely this was a working lunch.

'Do you think they'll go for the op?' she asked, and Gib frowned at her, as if he didn't understand the question.

'Josh and Maria,' she clarified, though why he needed clarification she didn't know. 'Which way do you think they'll jump?'

He studied her for a moment, an emotion she couldn't read clouding his usually clear blue eyes, then he gave a little shrug, as if casting off whatever it was he'd been thinking.

'They'll wait,' he said, no doubt in his voice.

'But when Josh asked you what you thought, you said we might have to operate—that there might be no choice. It seemed to me he took that to mean an op was inevitable.'

Gib nodded, then he smiled at her, and she felt a wistful longing that this might have been other than a working lunch.

Nonsense, she chided silently, picking up the thread of what he was saying and following his reasoning.

'But when he asked you the same question,' Gib continued, 'you said they didn't need to decide right now. That we were giving them the information because it might become a life-or-death decision and they should know the possible outcomes so they'd be prepared.'

'So?'

'So Maria was looking at the photo of Mackenzie as you answered. I don't think she wants her baby suffering any more.'

Oh!

All pretence that this could be anything other than a working lunch disappeared, and Sophie closed her eyes, praying the tears pricking at her eyelids would go away. She knew she should be over crying for babies by now, but had accepted that would never happen.

Gib seemed to understand, for he said, 'We would be failing them if we didn't feel for them.'

'Thanks,' she said quietly, then sat back so the waitress could put her meal down.

They ate in silence, but it was an easy quiet that lay between them—seductively easy, as she could get used to sitting like this with Gib, but deceptively easy as well, for just so could she slip into the way of thinking something might happen between them.

Look at that ring, she told herself. Any time you start thinking nonsense, just check it out.

'Blake Smith's doing well. Will you move him into the general care nursery before he goes home?'

'I talked to his parents when I came in this morning. Suggested they might like to spend the night in the private room, tending him themselves but with the staff as back-up. I'd prefer to do that. They're very young, and although I'm confident they're committed to giving him the best possible start they can, it might freak them out, doing everything for him that first twenty-four hours.'

'Nice medical term, freak them out,' Sophie teased, and Gib smiled at her.

'You know what I mean!'

'First sign of apnoea and, yes, I know exactly what you mean, but they get such good training and support. I saw young Todd gently rocking Blake the other day, and when I walked past he said "apnoea" to me as if he'd known for ever that babies could forget to breathe.'

'They'll take a monitor home with them, but it's good to use that first within the hospital confines, so they know what noise to expect and will learn whether the shriek of the monitor will jolt him into breathing again.'

'There's always something, isn't there?' Sophie said, feeling sorry for the young couple who were about to embark on the sole care of their tiny baby son.

'They'll manage,' Gib assured her, and she was confident, with this couple at least, that he was right. As far as Todd and Jenny were concerned, there was no such thing as too much information and they were prepared to put in the time to give young Blake every chance to catch up with his age group.

Was it coincidence that the first people she saw on her return to the unit were Todd and Jenny?

'We're staying the night then taking him home in the morning,' Jenny announced, her eyes bright with excitement. 'Tonight it will just be me and Todd, but once we get home Todd's mum's going to come over every afternoon, so I can have a sleep. Todd's got to go back to work, you see.'

Sophie wished the young parents all the best, then, after checking that all the babies, even Mackenzie, appeared content, she went down to see Thomas, hoping he'd have had his sleep and she could play with him for a while.

The hug he gave her was every bit as good as she'd imagined it would be, and the delight in his eyes when he realised she could stay for a while made her feel guilty that her job took her away from him at all. But as he drifted from playing just with her to playing with his friends, she was grateful he was secure enough in her love for him to be left in child care or with Etty without any adverse effects.

'He's a great kid,' Vicki said to her when, after a long goodbye hug, Sophie was returning to work. 'He's fitted in so well.'

Into my life, too, Sophie thought as the cold dread of the question she didn't want to consider seized her heart with icy fingers.

But Hilary had said the father wasn't interested. She had been so definite about it, Sophie had demanded to know if she'd told the man she was pregnant.

'I promised not to,' Hilary had said—a strange kind of remark, followed up by an even stranger one. 'And he promised he'd never ask.'

This was Sophie's dilemma. In seeking out Thomas's father, was she breaking Hilary's promise to him?

Yet, with her mother already instigating court proceedings to take Thomas from her, she needed this unknown man's support.

With a sigh that came up from the tips of her toes, she entered the lift, knowing by the time she reached the fifth floor where the NICU was located her mind had to be one hundred per cent focussed on her work. She could—and did—worry about Thomas in her own time, but the babies on the fifth floor deserved the best that she could give them…

CHAPTER FIVE

FRIDAY afternoon and Sophie gladly handed over responsibility of the NICU to Yui Lin, now officially pregnant,
and a paediatric registrar Gib had poached from one of the
other teams. The registrar would be on call all weekend,
Yui on duty for the next two nights.

Little Mackenzie was holding her own—in fact, Sophie
felt she was improving, which wouldn't be the case if her
bowel had perforated. They were putting her sudden
collapse the previous night down to sepsis—an infection
picked up somewhere along the line, but not necessarily
originating in her damaged intestines.

'You've been worrying us all to death,' she told the little
girl, stopping by her crib before she left the unit.

'You can say that again,' Josh, who was beside his
daughter, said. 'Maria is catching up on some sleep. You
look as if you could do with some as well.'

Sophie didn't argue but, tired as she was after two nights
on call, sleeping at the hospital in case she was needed,
computerising patient files whenever she had free time, she
felt her spirits lift as she headed for the child-care centre
to collect Thomas. They'd had so little time together this
week, and though he obviously loved Etty and was thriving

under her care, Sophie had missed his hugs and sloppy kisses—even his unanswerable questions.

'He's in with the big kids,' Vicki greeted her when she walked in. 'They've got a visitor and as Thomas knows him he went along as well.'

Thomas knows him? Sophie's stomach muscles clenched. She wanted to shout at Vicki, tell her strangers should never be allowed inside, but Vicki was ahead of her.

'He's a regular visitor,' she said. 'All the kids love him.'

By this time Sophie was at the doorway of the pre-school area and could see the visitor. Though how someone as tall as Gib could fold himself onto a four-year-old-size chair she didn't know.

His back was to her, his hands busy with a mess of play dough, modelling a figure of some kind. The children around the table were similarly employed, although Thomas seemed to be eating his rather than making something with it.

The stomach muscles that had relaxed when she saw who the 'visitor' was now began to tense again. Why was he here?

'Sophie!'

Thomas's glad cry thrust away the remnants of her concern and she spread her arms as he ran towards her. It also made Gib turn and he held up hands green from the play dough and grinned at her.

'Come and join us,' he said, as Sophie scooped a hurtling Thomas into her arms and hugged him tight, pressing her cheek against his bouncing curls, feeling the little skip of her heart produced by the deep love she felt for him, and heightened by fear that she might lose him.

'Yes, come and make something, Sophie!' Thomas added his own plea. 'And see Gib's pig. He makes the best pigs.'

'It was supposed to be a donkey,' Gib explained, as Sophie drew cautiously closer. 'We were doing a nativity scene.'

'I'm sure there were pigs somewhere in the vicinity,' Sophie said, hoping she sounded OK when the unexpectedness of this encounter was now making her distinctly nervous.

Tiredness?

She thought not...

Thomas squiggled out of her arms and returned to the table, tugging her by the hand so she had no choice but to take the empty chair beside Gib and examine the animals he and the other children had already completed.

'You can do the donkey,' he said to her, passing her a ball of slightly dirty red play dough.

The children showed their models, and argued over whose was best—Thomas insisting his nibbled-at oblong was a sheep. Then, the limit of his attention span reached, he drifted off with two other boys, the three of them turning their animals into battering rams as they charged at each other.

'What are you doing here?' Sophie asked, keeping her voice below the level of the children's chatter.

Gib smiled at her.

'It must seem odd, but I often come down and play with the kids for a while. I think that's how Etty started her volunteering here. It's the normality of it I like.'

The explanation stopped there, and from the sure way his fingers moved, shaping a green lump into something that might have been a person, she knew his attention was back on his task, not their conversation.

'Normality?'

He looked up now, as if surprised by her query.

'I suppose, having Thomas, it doesn't mean as much to you, but because most, if not all, of the children I have dealings with were either preemies or low birth weight babies, their progress is different. I know we have charts and tables that give us detailed standards of development of so-called normal children, but they're figures and graphs, not real life children. It's one thing to read that by three or four a child will represent a human figure with hands and feet and hair, but it's different to see them doing it.'

'You come down here to watch them draw?'

'And play!' Gib said, putting down his model and turning so he was looking directly at her. 'The point is, I see kids who began life in the NICU growing and developing, learning new skills, and I get excited for them and for their parents, but it's hard to judge how far they still have to go unless you see them with children of their age group. Look at this lot—see Sally over there, and Sam, her twin. They were low birth weight babies, and although they are socially OK with children of their own age, seeing them with the others, making models, drawing, even in pretend play, you can see where those two are still catching up.'

Sophie understood what he was saying but her attention had shifted to Thomas and, seeing him playing so well with the two older boys, she smiled.

'He's a very well-adjusted child,' Gib said, apparently following her eyes if not her thoughts. 'At his age, I'd have been like Aaron over there.'

He pointed to a small child standing a little apart, smiling at the three boys' play but not joining in.

'Only I'd have been sucking my first two fingers as I watched.'

'Bit of a loner?' Sophie asked, turning back to look at him, seeing, as he lifted his left hand to indicate which fingers he'd sucked, that he was no longer wearing his wedding ring.

Because of the play dough catching in it?

'You could say that!' he said, his ringless hand busy again with the little figure.

Thomas returned to her side and, anxious to be alone with him—or anxious not to be so close to Gib?—Sophie stood up.

'I'll see you later,' Gib said. 'Etty phoned earlier to say as we'd all be home together, we might have a barbeque. We can have it early so it won't affect Thomas's bedtime too severely.'

Sophie stared at him.

'You don't like barbeques?' Gib prompted. 'You're not one of those people who think charred meat is carcinogenic?'

'It is, isn't it? However, barbeques don't worry me, but if you've got a night off, surely you've got better things to do than cook a barbeque for me and Thomas.'

Especially if you're still a loner!

'And Etty,' he reminded her. 'And I'm not committing to an entire night of barbequing. So, see you at home?'

He smiled and Sophie knew all the warnings she'd been giving herself about not being attracted to this man had failed. His smile made her toes tingle, and her heart tap out a rap rhythm against her ribs. She felt hot and cold all at the same time, and although she knew Thomas was talking to her—tugging at her hand and saying something—her ears had tuned him out, Gib's final sentence—*See you at home*—echoing over and over again in her head.

'Or it will be too late for a swim.'

Thomas's voice finally penetrated the fog in which she found herself, although it was Gib who answered the little boy.

'It's never too late for a swim in our pool, Thomas,' he

said. 'There are lights all around it, and even under the water so you can see really well in there at night.'

'Lights under the water? Did you hear that, Sophie? Can we swim at night? Can we swim tonight?'

With or without Alexander Gibson?

He wasn't committing for an entire night so maybe he was going out. Maybe he had a date. Maybe that was why he'd taken off his wedding ring.

Sophie considered all these things as she led Thomas to the car and clipped him into his car seat. It was better than considering how she'd feel if Gib *did* swim with them. If the man, fully clothed, could make her toes tingle with a smile, what would seeing him half-naked do to her extremities?

Give her goose bumps! She found that out a couple of hours later, when Gib decreed it was dark enough for the pool lights to go on and Thomas insisted they all have a swim.

All but Etty, who announced she'd had enough swims for one day and would be better employed fixing salads for the barbeque and making a cherry tart for sweets.

Thomas was already in the pool, getting through the water with his fearless dog-paddling motion, and Gib had dived in the deep end and was swimming lazy laps. Sophie hesitated to take off the sarong wrap she had tied at her waist, as embarrassed and uncertain about revealing her body as she'd been when she'd first developed breasts.

Would he think her too thin?

As if it mattered!

'Come on Sophie!' Thomas called, and she whipped off the sarong and slid into the water. Perhaps if she stayed submerged, her body size and shape wouldn't be too obvious.

Thomas splashed water at her face, reminding her the

issue was his happiness, not Alexander Gibson's impression of her body. She splashed back and soon forgot everything but the sheer joy of playing in the water with her little boy.

Her little boy! Fiercely she echoed the words, renewing her determination to fight for the right to keep him—fight her mother and, if necessary, his father, too.

Whoever he might be!

Gib hauled himself out of the water at the far end of the pool and watched them play, seeing the joy in both their faces, seeing Sophie's hair escaping from the knot at the back of her head, dark threads of it lying wetly on her back.

Was he becoming obsessed by Sophie's hair?

Definitely not—his attention was just as easily attracted to the pale, slim body he could see beneath the water. She was wearing a black swimsuit that clung to her shapely breasts and slender waist, before following the swell of her hips.

His left thumb moved to his ring finger of that hand and he realised he'd forgotten to put his wedding ring back on after playing with the play dough.

Forgotten?

'Gib, watch me swim to you.'

Thomas's cry was a timely reminder that he shouldn't be thinking of Sophie the way he was, and he watched the little boy swim splashily towards him. He was a cute little kid, so confident and full of life. It had only been a week since he had moved in, but Gib was enjoying getting to know him.

Thomas reached him and Gib slid into the water. He lifted the child onto his shoulders, feeling the lack of weight—the slightness of his body—and felt a rush of something he didn't understand as small fingers grasped his hair. Suddenly he found himself thinking, for the first time in years, about Hilary Cooper, and whether or not she'd conceived.

If maybe, somewhere, he had a child…

But that was neither here nor there. Being a dad was out of the question—of course he liked kids, but he'd made the decision not to be a father. Not only that, he'd made a promise.

'Go under, Gib, go under!' Thomas yelled, and Gib ducked under so both he and the little boy were submerged momentarily before bobbing back up to the surface.

'Did you see, Sophie! Did you see?'

Gib lifted the child down, turned his eel-slippery form in his arms and set him swimming back to Sophie.

He couldn't get attached to Thomas. Sophie would move on—meet someone who'd be only too happy to take Thomas as part of the package. Yet as Thomas turned again and splashed back towards him, so confident Gib's arms would reach out to hold him, that strange feeling returned.

The barbeque was set up down by the river in a gazebo with a long table of iron lace and matching chairs with bright yellow cushions to soften the seats. Sophie sat so her arm rested on the low wall of the gazebo and looked out at the river, the aroma of sizzling steak tantalising her taste buds while Thomas's chatter, as he 'helped' Gib cook, made her warm with happiness.

OK, so thinking about Gib made her warm in other ways, but she could cope with that, as long as Thomas was safe and happy.

'Do you think you've got enough food?' she asked Etty, who'd been setting the table and putting out dishes of salad while they swam.

'Wait till you see Gib eat,' Etty told her. 'He might

look lean and mean but that man can put away a mountain of food.'

'That man' appeared in person, carrying a platter of steaks, Thomas following importantly behind with the barbeque tongs.

We could almost be a family, Sophie thought, then she glanced at Gib's left hand to remind herself he was still in love with his dead wife.

The ring was still missing.

Had he forgotten to put it back on?

Or had her earlier guess been correct and he'd taken it off because he was going out with someone later—someone he felt serious enough about to finally remove the ring?

The smell of the meat turned from tempting and delicious to distinctly nauseating, but Sophie forced herself to choose a small piece for Thomas, cutting it up for him, adding salad to his plate, then passing it across the table.

Etty was chattering about the Christmas decorations she and Thomas would put up tomorrow, asking Gib if he'd be available to help with the high bits, although they wouldn't need him for the angel for the top of the tree until the following week.

'It's due to be delivered next Saturday.'

'Just how big is this tree you've ordered?' Gib asked, and Sophie, seeing the fondness in his eyes as he spoke to Etty, felt a surge of jealousy towards the unknown woman for whom Gib had removed his ring.

'It's very very big.' Thomas answered for Etty, holding his little arms as wide as they would go. 'Me and Etty, we meas—' He looked towards his carer who smiled and offered him the word he needed. 'Measured to the roof and got one that big.'

'*That* big?' Gib teased, and Sophie's jealousy morphed to regret. He was so *nice*, this boss of hers—nice all the way through that he'd bother with a little boy he barely knew and allow what apparently was a monstrous tree to be set up in his lovely house.

No wonder she was falling—

Don't even think about it!

She ate her meal, knowing it was delicious and she should be appreciating it more, but too tied up in thoughts of Gib to do more than chew and swallow.

'A certain small boy looks ready for bed,' Etty said, and Sophie stood up, glad of an excuse to get away from the cosy family atmosphere that had crept around them.

'No, you sit, I'll take him,' Etty insisted. 'We're halfway through a story we want to finish, aren't we, Thomas?'

Sophie hesitated but as Thomas came towards her for a goodnight kiss, then went off happily on Etty's knee, she couldn't argue.

'I'm sorry,' Gib said, when the pair had disappeared into the shadows of the house that loomed above them.

Sorry?

'For what?' Sophie asked, turning to face him although she'd been trying to avoid looking at him.

'For Etty. She's about as subtle as a sledgehammer. Taking Thomas like that—leaving the two of us together. She thinks I should remarry and now you're here, with a little boy she already adores, she can't believe I haven't snapped you up.'

'In a little over a week?' Sophie said lightly, although her heart was racing and her breathing mechanism had gone awry. 'And you? How do you feel? Do *you* want to remarry?'

Another head-slapping moment! Had she really asked that?

But before she'd died of shame, he answered.

'No.'

One definite word, which should have stopped her cold, but caution didn't stand a chance.

'That's it? Just no? Presumably you've a reason.'

He chuckled, as if her persistent—pathetic?—probing was amusing him. But when he stood up and walked towards the fence that separated his property from the river, his shoulders were slumped and his head bowed, body language suggesting there was nothing amusing about his reason.

Regret that she'd upset him made her move towards him, desperate to offer comfort—or at least make amends.

'I'm sorry. It's none of my business. I don't know why I kept asking.'

He glanced towards her, then, as if feeling her empathy, he put his arm around her shoulders and drew her closer, so they both stood leaning against the fence, looking out at the river.

'A man and a woman, softly lapping water, the moon shining on the river—why wouldn't you be asking?'

He looked down into her face, and Sophie, in wonderment that the connection between them had suddenly shifted to a whole new dimension, held her breath. Then he lifted his hand and pulled out the comb that held her damp hair knotted, probably untidily, behind her head.

'I've been wanting to do that for days,' he murmured. 'And this.'

He ran his fingers through her freed hair and fanned it out so it fell across her back and shoulders.

'Beautiful hair, beautiful smile—how could a man walk away from you, Sophie? Or did you walk, taking Thomas with you?'

Sophie stilled. 'He didn't walk away because we were never together and he never wanted Thomas. He doesn't even know he exists. But that's not the point. We were talking about you, so don't think changing the subject will divert me.'

He was staring down into the water that slid so quietly past them.

'If he doesn't know, how do you know he doesn't want Thomas?'

It was the question striking fear in Sophie's heart, and she shivered as she used Hilary's words—the words kept her going these days.

'It was agreed he'd have nothing to do with Thomas,' she said.

Had he noticed her slight, involuntary shudder that he touched her again—touched her shoulder and, moving closer, smoothed her hair?

'The man's a fool,' he muttered, more to himself than to her, then he turned her so she was facing him, and with one hand tilted her head so he could look into her eyes.

'This attraction between us, do you feel it, too?'

She dipped her head in reluctant agreement, too uptight and anxious to find words to confirm or—more sensibly—deny it.

But that barely there nod was all the answer he needed, for he bent his head and brushed an, oh, so gentle kiss across her lips.

She pushed away before her feelings could betray her—not far away, but out of kissing distance.

'I, ah... There's Thomas. I...'

What on earth was she supposed to say?

Well, for a start she could ask why, if he didn't want to remarry, he'd taken off his wedding ring, her sensible self replied, but standing close to him, feeling the heat of his body, was so good she didn't want to spoil the moment.

'I've been wanting to do that, too,' he said softly. 'But now it's done, that's as far as it goes, sweet Sophie. I don't get involved—too involved—with women any more, particularly not with women who have to consider their child before they go into a relationship.'

'Presumably you've a reason,' Sophie said, moving far enough away from him to ease the physical chaos his body was causing.

He'd turned towards the river again, and she knew he'd withdrawn inside himself—tucking the part that was attracted to her safely away in some distant corner of his psyche.

'I let my wife down—not once but many times.'

At first the words made no sense at all, then, as a coolness swept through Sophie's body, she realised he was answering the question she'd asked earlier—giving her a reason for his avoidance of involvement.

'Gillian was everything I wasn't. She was beautiful, bright, vivacious, an extrovert to my introvert. She was an actress, working in television—in serial dramas made in Melbourne or Sydney—so she was away during the week for most of each year.'

Silence fell between them, a silence so tensely uncomfortable Sophie felt she had to break it.

'That must have been hard on your marriage.'

Gib turned to her as if surprised, and shook his head.

'It wasn't, you know. In fact, if anything, it made things more exciting.'

Exciting? The description made Sophie even more tense.

'We'd meet again each weekend as if it was for the first time, and for years I thought the magic would never go away.'

Magic?

Another knot formed in Sophie's stomach. How could an ordinary woman like herself compete with magic?

'So for years I didn't realise the excitement—her gaiety—wasn't natural. That more often than not I was seeing Gillian's highs and somehow missing the lows, although in those early days of her illness the lows weren't as extreme as they became later, when often she was hospitalised for months before drugs could balance the chemicals in her brain and she could handle life again.'

Pity for the woman and for the husband who had so obviously loved her made Sophie forget her own reaction and move close again, resting her hand on Gib's arm in an unspoken show of sympathy.

'In those early days, if she was home, not working, I put the lows down to me being busy—she was missing my company because I was either studying, or working all hours of the day and night. It was natural she might be depressed.'

Sophie heard his huff of self-disgust, and pity for him—and for poor, tortured Gillian—made her eyes sting with tears as he muttered savagely, 'I was a doctor, for heaven's sake, and I couldn't diagnose my own wife with a bipolar condition!'

'I don't remember much from my psych lectures, because I always knew I wanted to work with kids, but would that have made a difference?' Sophie asked, hoping to ease the pain she heard in his voice. 'Would getting her on drugs earlier have improved the long-term outcome?'

He didn't answer, but after a minute he put his hand on hers and squeezed her fingers gently.

'Probably not,' he admitted, and though they stood together—touching—Sophie knew she could have been anyone, male or female—just someone who happened to be around when Gib decided the time had come to talk about his marriage.

'When we were first married, I wanted a child—a number of children—but it would have interrupted Gillian's career at a time it was just beginning to take off. Then later, when she wanted a child, I wasn't so sure about it—about whether she would be able to cope, especially if, by chance, the child had special needs. We talked about it and decided we wouldn't have children, but although she agreed it was a sensible decision, I wondered afterwards if she'd just agreed to placate me. Was she disappointed that her condition worsened? Again, I don't know, but it was about that time that she was first hospitalised. Then it was as if our world went mad. Little things became hugely important to her, chance remarks took on dreadful connotations, and she saw my love for her as something bad—even evil. As her health, physical as well as mental, deteriorated, I brought Etty to live with us, and Gillian hated that as well—hated that she had what, in her bad times, she called a gaoler.'

He sighed, then added, 'I doubt, in retrospect, I ever made a right decision for her and that, Sophie, is what I have to live with. But I live with it alone—I wouldn't foist it on another woman, or put myself into a position where I could make the same mistakes all over again.'

Silence, then the final nail in Sophie's coffin of hopes. 'Or new mistakes.'

He touched her lightly on the top of her head and moved away, picking up a big plastic box from beside the barbeque and beginning to stack the detritus of their meal into it.

She should offer to help, but if she went into the light, would he see traces of the tears she'd wept for him, and for his beautiful, tortured, childless Gillian?

'I'll take this up to the house and start the dishwasher,' he said, as if the conversation and the kisses had never happened. 'You'll be all right down here? Find your way back up to the house when you're ready. If you want to swim, the lights are still on in the pool.'

Sophie nodded, not trusting her voice, but she didn't want to swim, or go back to her lonely bedroom in the flat. She wanted to stay here by the river.

With Gib.

A man and a woman and moonlight and water lapping...

Foolish as it was, she wanted the magic of romance, with a man who had been so badly burnt by it, he no longer believed in it.

CHAPTER SIX

'LIKE to do a retrieval flight?'

The weekend had passed too quickly, Sophie spending most of it with Thomas, taking him on the City Cats that plied the river, first to Southbank where they swam then further down the river for a picnic in a large, tree-shaded park.

When he rested, or played quietly in the flat, she'd phoned the friends Hilary had made while working at the research institute in Brisbane. Some she'd already spoken to, needing their help to organise the memorial service for her sister, but others were just names in Hilary's address book until she made the phone calls and heard them talk of her sister with respect and affection.

Through these people, Hilary's friends and colleagues, Sophie was certain she would find Thomas's father.

On Sunday afternoon, Gib had found her and Thomas in the pool, and had suggested a barbeque, but, still twitchy from their weird conversation after Friday's barbeque, Sophie had declined, saying she'd promised Thomas she'd take him out for a burger.

Which was true, although she hadn't specified a day!

Now, with Thomas safely tucked into bed, and a weekend of avoiding Gib successfully completed, Sophie wandered back down to the lower terrace and stood by the river, watching it slide by, lapping softly at the rocks. She touched her fingers against her lips, brushing them as lightly as Gib's kiss had brushed them, and, remembering, dreamt foolish dreams.

'Sophie, can you hear me? Would you like to do a re-trieval flight?'

Gib was calling to her from the living-room window and something in his voice suggested it wasn't the first time he'd called. How long had she been mooning by the river?

'Triplets born only four weeks premature but low birth weights, two hours' flight west of Brisbane.'

'I'm on my way—five minutes to get changed and I'll be ready to go.'

She took the steps up from the lower terrace two at a time, pulling off her sarong as she went, aware of how easy having Etty around had made her working life.

'Do you normally do transport flights?' she asked when she joined him in the car. 'And do you usually take two doctors?'

'No and no. Haven't done a flight for years, but with the staff shortage, well, when the flight co-ordinator phoned to advise me it was on, I thought, Why not?'

'Then you thought what a good opportunity to see how the new girl handles herself, so I'm going instead of, what? An NICU nurse? I can't imagine you'd leave the respira-tory therapist behind.'

They were on the main road now, well lit enough for Sophie to see the smile playing around Gib's lips.

'Close, but it's not a test of your skill or ability—I've seen enough of your work to know the glowing references you provided were all true. But the co-ordinator hadn't phoned a nurse and I realised it would be a good opportunity for you to see how our transport team works. The Royal Flying Doctor Service has a plane based in Brisbane and for longer flights we use that if it's available. If it's not, there's a government jet. The RFDS plane is best because of its configuration, but the two infant transport incubators we use have self-contained power supplies to maintain the thermal environment, ventilators, temp and cardio monitoring, oxygen and compressed air, suction devices and infusion pumps, so they can go into helicopters, ambulances—whatever vehicle is required.'

They were travelling through a part of the city Sophie didn't recognise, although bright lights ahead suggested they were close to the airport.

'Thirty minutes—that's the mobilisation time we aim for.'

He'd taken a side street that led to a security gate, which was already opening as if the guard knew the car.

'The co-ordinator advises airport security of our number plates,' Gib explained, lifting a hand in thanks to the man and driving through rows of long hangars, towards a well-lit apron. 'As you guessed, we'll have a respiratory therapist—you're replacing a nurse.'

He was parking the car when something he'd said earlier registered in Sophie's brain.

'Two transport incubators? Aren't there three babies?'

He turned and smiled, making her forget this was work, not pleasure.

'I'll put all three in together in one if I can. Have you been doing that in Sydney? Keeping twins together in one crib? We've found they seem to like each other's company, and will lie quietly together for longer waking periods than when they're kept apart. We haven't done a formal study of it, but are talking to other NICUs about the possibility of keeping data.'

Why had he asked her to come?

That was the question persisting in Gib's head as he watched the way Sophie cocked her head slightly when she was listening—watched how her hair, this evening loosely pulled back into a ponytail, swished across one shoulder as she did it.

'We've done it in our ICU if the babies have much the same needs, although with multiple births there's usually one that has done less well *in utero*,' she said, showing him she was far more focussed on the job than he was.

He led the way to the waiting plane, knowing from the way she greeted Sue, the respiratory therapist, that they'd met before. The pilot introduced himself and showed Gib how he'd secured the incubators and medical bags, which had arrived by ambulance minutes earlier. He then explained the flight details, asked them to strap in, and within minutes they were taxiing across the tarmac.

'Are other flights cleared for us?' Sophie asked.

'Usually,' Sue responded. 'They won't abort the take-off or landing of another plane, but once the tower is advised we've got a mission, they work the flight times to fit us in.'

'The plane could be going to retrieve a donated organ, or a critically injured road accident victim, so there has to be prioritising,' Gib added, wondering how it was possible for his head to be carrying two parallel lines of thought—the one work-focussed, the other seeing Sophie's pink, unpainted lips and thinking how they'd tasted in that all-too-brief kiss.

Was he wrong to assume she wouldn't want a short-term relationship?

Were the babies being kept warm?

She hadn't reacted to the kiss but, then, it had barely been a kiss...

Would all three babies fit in one incubator?

'Sue was telling me about the quads she helped transport last year.'

Gib turned to Sophie.

'She was saying you lost one.'

'Thirty-four weeks gestation and all less than one thousand grams,' Gib said, hoping memories of the quads would force his mind onto one track. 'The smallest fellow had PDA—common enough with all premature babies, but with him we couldn't get the darned duct to close with medication and even after surgery he was getting leakage of blood from his aorta back into his lungs. This led, of course, to increased fluid in his lungs, heart having to work harder—the poor wee thing went from one problem to another.'

Sophie studied him for a moment, as if those smoky grey eyes were trying to peer beneath his skin.

'It doesn't matter how many babies you lose, does it? Each one is still like a knife wound in your heart,' she said softly.

'You feel that?'

His surprise must have shown, for she frowned at him. 'You don't?'

He shook his head at the thought that he might, one day, not feel that stab of agony in his heart.

'I do,' he admitted, 'but I've met plenty of professionals who feel it's for the best, or are content that they have done whatever they could and so the end result is nothing to do with them.'

'I think they still care,' Sophie retorted. 'They just say

things like that to cover up the sense of loss that is some-times so swamping you wonder why you do the job.'

'Until a healthy fifteen-year-old walks into your con-sulting room, kisses your cheek and announces she's going to study medicine because of you.'

'Has that actually happened to you?'

'Becky Wainwright,' Sue said, nodding towards Sophie as she supplied the young woman's name. 'She came in the week before you started. Gosh, she was small at birth, wasn't she, Gib?'

'Teenage mother, smoker, thought she was getting fat so she'd dieted like mad. Becky was only a week prema-ture but so small everyone doubted she'd survive. But she was tough, and her mother was tougher. She totally turned her life around, went back to school, got into university, studied child care and you'd know her as Vicki—Thomas's teacher in the centre downstairs.'

'That's a wonderful story. I must talk to Vicki about how she managed. She must have had good family help.'

A tightness in Sophie's voice as she made the offhand remark made Gib wonder about her family circumstances. But Thomas was only three. Sophie would have been thirty—and a fully fledged paediatrician—when she had him. The parallels between her and Vicki were hardly relevant.

Except that, like Vicki, she was raising a child on her own...

Sue had gone forward to sit with the pilot and, though Gib knew it was none of his business, he found himself asking.

'You didn't have family help with Thomas?'

Sophie looked at him, her eyes widening.

'I barely had a family—just my sister and my gran. And they're both dead.'

She turned away, peering out the window into the blackness. What was it about this man that he could touch the sore parts of her so unerringly?

Or had her attraction to him, pointless though it was, sensitised her in some way?

'OK, folks, strap in tight, there's a storm ahead but I'll try to go around it. Sue's up here with me, so it's just you two back there.'

The pilot's voice was tinny, but that didn't make the warning any less effective. Sophie pulled at her seat-belt strap to make sure it was tight, and not a minute too soon, for the plane dipped one wing then bucked and dropped, with stomach-heaving suddenness, through the air. It levelled out again, but not before Sophie had grabbed for Gib's hand, needing to anchor herself to another human being, rather than just the arm of her seat.

Everything beyond survival forgotten, Sophie clung to him, willing the storm to pass—or the pilot to go even further from its power. Beyond the windows, lightning lit the sky with a fierce glow, showing the dark clouds boiling up and up, beyond and below them.

'Nice adventure?' Gib said calmly, and Sophie scowled at him.

'I hate planes,' she muttered, miles beyond diplomacy now. 'Hate, hate, hate them!'

'You didn't have to come.' He spoke so mildly she could feel her teeth grinding together as she fought to hang onto her temper.

'Of course I did,' she snapped, letting go the reins just a little. 'Doing transport runs is part of my job. I can't get picky about the form of transport.'

She paused then added, 'But I don't have to enjoy it!'

He squeezed her fingers. How mortifying to find she was still gripping his hand while she showed how cowardly she was about plane travel. She pulled her fingers free, but the plane lurched again, and she grasped for him again, her hand landing on his leg, her fingers pressing in so tightly she was probably bruising him.

'Want a distraction?'

His fingers were moving in her hair and the three words, barely audible above the engine noise, insinuated themselves into her ears. She turned towards him and saw how close he was—saw his blue eyes looking intently at her, his gaze sliding from her eyes towards her lips.

Lips that were suddenly so dry she had to lick them.

'Imagine it,' he whispered, touching his own tongue to his upper lip. 'Lips meeting, heat building, imagine that nothing kiss we shared going further, Sophie.'

Had he hypnotised her that she could actually feel his lips on hers—taste his tongue as it teased against her teeth? She knew her breath was coming faster, her heart rate rising as she felt the kiss that wasn't a kiss grow more and more demanding. His fingers massaged the back of her neck, beneath the band that kept her hair contained, and a subtle pressure was bringing her head towards him, although she was ninety-nine per cent certain he had no intention of taking it further than talk.

Distraction! That's all it was.

'Do you want to feel my heart beating? Feel how you affect me when we're only imagining a kiss?'

She did and yet she didn't, but then he lifted her hand off his leg and held it against his shirt so she could, indeed, feel the rapid thudding of his heart.

The plane lurched again, but the movement didn't

bother her, for now Gib's forefinger was tracing the line of her lips—parted lips, dragging in great gulps of air. Then his finger slid into her mouth, and she licked its saltiness, then heard him gasp as she closed her lips around it, and sucked on it—gently, oh, so gently…

Had they missed the storm?

How much time had passed during what she now felt to be a dream sequence of some kind?

Surely no more than seconds, yet that bump Sophie felt was definitely the wheels touching down on a runway, and the braking of the plane was forcing her against her seat belt. She pulled her hand away from Gib, turning her face so he wouldn't see her embarrassment.

'Sorry about that, folks!' the pilot said cheerily when, with the plane now stationary, he came back into the cabin to open the door for them. 'Storm season—we get to expect a few bumpy rides.'

Sophie unclipped her seat belt and stood up, grateful to be able to stretch—eager to get out of the plane, eager to get away from Gib—but as she reached the top of the steps she saw the ambulance pulled up as close as it could get, one of the ambos already opening the rear door.

'Let them bring the babies in,' Gib said quietly. 'We'll stabilise them once they're on board.'

The ambulanceman had pulled a stretcher out, the wheeled supports dropping to the ground. On it sat a man, a sheet bundled around him.

'I've got them all,' he said. 'The nurse at the hospital said this was the best way to keep them warm.'

The ambulanceman stood behind the man as he negotiated the steps into the plane then helped him sit down. It was only then Sophie realised he was cradling all three babies against his skin—kangaroo care—but although it was practised in most hospitals if the baby's condition allowed, she'd never seen a man with three babies held firmly against his chest.

Eager hands reached out to relieve him of his burdens but, like any new father, he was reluctant to let go.

'That one's Kristie,' he said, as Sue took the first baby and settled her in the incubator. 'She came first.'

Sophie took the next one, murmuring hello to little Carly, settling her, at Gib's behest, beside her sister in the crib.

'And this is Angus.' Fatherly pride shone in the man's eyes and reverberated in his voice as he handed his precious son to Gib. 'We know we can't travel to Brisbane with you, but just as soon as the nurse says Helen—that's my wife—can travel, we'll be on our way by road.'

Relieved of the babies, he now stood up, buttoning his shirt, the cotton blanket that had been wrapped around his chest left forgotten on the ground. He was too anxious to see what was happening. He watched as Gib slid a catheter into the stub of Angus's umbilical cord so they had a port for fluid or drugs, and Sophie did the same for Carly and Kristie then attached monitors to the babies' chests. Sue counted respirations, tiny tubes close to hand in case one or all of then needed intubation.

'You'll call them by their names?' the father said anxiously, as Gib fastened small-size identity bracelets onto the babies' skinny legs.

'We will,' Sophie assured him, 'and we'll take special care of them. You get back to Helen—she'll be fretting, and anxious to know how they travelled. And drive safely—these little people need you both.'

The man touched his children again, one big, calloused forefinger pressing against each forehead as if in benediction. Then he said a hoarsely uttered goodbye to each in turn—by name—and Sophie had to swallow hard to remove the lump in her throat.

'I wonder why the names were so important to him,' Sue asked, when the babies were settled and the plane once again in the air.

'Maybe because there were three of them,' Gib suggested. 'He didn't want us getting them muddled.'

'It seemed more than that,' Sophie said. 'He had a bit of an accent. Maybe when he came from his home country he had to change his name.'

Speculation over names, then over the babies' status, kept them occupied for the much smoother ride back to Brisbane, Sophie relaxing enough to think she might end up enjoying plane travel if she had to do it often. Though it was unlikely she'd ever be travelling with Gib again—or with his unusual method of distraction.

She pushed away the thought, then forgot the interlude altogether for by the time they reached the hospital little Angus was suffering bradycardia, his heart rate dropping down to seventy.

The might of science took over and the little boy was X-rayed and scanned, but no cardiac abnormalities, apart from PDA—a fairly normal condition for preemies—were found, and though he seemed to be having periods of apnoea when he stopped breathing, and apnoea could cause bradycardia, it didn't seem likely this would have caused his heart rate to slow so dramatically.

'He was last born—could he have had some oxygen deprivation during his birth?' Sue asked Gib, as the three of them, reluctant to leave their charges until they knew they were safe, stood around Angus's crib in the NICU.

'That could cause other problems, mainly developmental ones, both physical and mental, but it shouldn't be slowing his heart rate now.'

Gib put his hand through the port as he spoke and gently massaged the tiny, underdeveloped chest.

'Come on, little guy,' he said. 'We promised your dad we'd look after you.'

'Come on, Angus,' Sophie corrected, her eyes flicking between the baby and the monitor screen, back and forth, willing something to happen that might change the baby's status.

His respiratory rate was good—fifty breaths a minute— so why was his heart so reluctant to beat? Heart problems, heart anomalies, even PDA, usually resulted in a faster heart rate as the heart speeded up its action in an attempt to right the imbalance the condition caused.

'Increase his oxygen,' Gib said to Sue when Angus's oximeter reading showed he wasn't getting enough oxygen into his blood.

Sophie glanced towards his sisters, spooned together in another isolette.

'Should we put him in with them?' she asked Gib, who shook his head.

'We tried him in with Carly—or was it Kristie?'

'Maybe the father was a twin and always called the wrong name,' Sophie told him. 'So now he's determined to get it right. It was Carly, but we didn't try him in with both of them. After all, the three of them have shared a small womb-sized space for the last nine months.'

Gib studied her for a minute, and she knew it wasn't personal—he was simply weighing up her idea.

'We can try it,' he said, and the nurse who'd been appointed to tend Angus lifted him carefully in her hands.

Both hands!

Sophie went ahead of her, shifting the other two babies slightly so Angus would fit between them.

The nurse set him down, then checked the leads were still hooked up to the monitor.

'Well, will you look at that?'

It was the nurse who pointed to the screen, but they could all see the improvement, Angus's heart beats picking up to eighty beats a minute in no time at all.

'We can't consider it a miracle and not keep a close eye on him,' Gib warned. 'Especially when the three are separated for feeds or treatment.'

He left the room, returning ten minutes later to find Sue and Sophie still hovering over the crib.

'Sue's on duty tonight, but you're not,' he reminded Sophie. 'Not for another…' he checked his watch '…four hours, so if you want to get some sleep before you start, I'll run you home.'

Sue looked a question at her, and Sophie explained, 'We live together,' then heard the words and hurried to explain. 'In a flat—I live in a separate flat, Thomas and I.'

As she and Sue had only ever exchanged work-related words, this explanation probably left Sue even more confused.

Or even more certain Sophie and Gib were having an affair?

Sophie was still squirming over her *faux pas* when Sue spoke again.

'Ah, Thomas!' she said. 'We've all been wondering if there was a man in your life. Was he from up here? Did you move from Sydney to be near him? What does he do?'

Sophie was about to explain exactly who Thomas was—or at least explain he was a child—when Gib forestalled her.

'If you start answering Sue's questions, you'll be here all night. Believe me, she won't be happy until she knows every little detail of your private life, and once Sue knows, the world will know.'

'Only the hospital world,' Sue protested, but her smile suggested she wasn't the least bit offended by Gib's words.

'Well, too bad, because Sophie and I are going home—me to Aunt Etty and Sophie to her Thomas, so make what you want of that.'

Gib took Sophie's elbow and steered her away from the triplets' crib.

'The entire neonatal staff are at one with Aunt Etty, and are always trying to fix me up with a date, or match me up with someone. You mentioning Thomas was brilliant. It threw Sue off completely.'

'But I was going to explain,' Sophie told him, moving away from him so his touch wasn't distracting her. 'It doesn't feel right, letting her think—'

'Does it worry you what people think?' Gib asked, stopping by his car and opening the door for her.

She looked into his face, unreadable in the shadowy light, and replied honestly.

'Not much. I mean, I'd hate for people to think I was a snob, or above myself, but I'm a fairly private person, not because I want to hide things but because I find it hard to talk about myself. I was brought up—'

What had happened to finding it hard to talk about

herself? she wondered, as she stopped the conversation just in time and slid into the car seat.

'You were brought up...?' he queried as they exited the car-park.

She studied his profile, wondering if he'd persist if she didn't answer. She guessed he wouldn't because he appeared to be just as private about his personal affairs as she was. The information he'd disclosed earlier—about his marriage—had sounded dry and dusty, as though it had been tucked away deep inside him for a very long time.

'Weren't we all?' she said lightly, and saw him smile.

But driving home with him was a mistake. The car enclosed them in a capsule of privacy, the cool air-conditioning, the leather smell of the seats, the river flowing by all contributing to the sensual...discomfort that built within Sophie's body. Try as she may to think of the babies, her mind was fixated on Gib's touch, his finger on her lips, her lips capturing it...

'You're far too young and attractive to have shut yourself away from life,' he said, as he turned the car off the main road towards his house. 'And suggesting you live here was probably a mistake.'

He pulled into the drive and Sophie turned to stare at him, although the trees allowed little moonlight to filter through, so she couldn't see him clearly in the shadowy darkness.

'You want us to move out?'

'No!'

The word snapped as abruptly as a slap towards her and she sat back in her seat, wondering just what he might be getting at.

'But it's wrong for you. You might feel awkward bringing home a date—a man. I've made it hard for you.'

Sophie shook her head. She knew she should let it go—should get out of the car, go into her flat and hope Gib had got rid of whatever bee he had in his bonnet by the time she saw him again.

But this man had held her in a sexual thrall—there was no other word for it—less than four hours ago, and now he was telling her to get lost.

Not that she wanted him, of course. She didn't want any man in her life—at least not until she'd sorted things out for Thomas. And even then she'd have to be extremely careful that any man she might choose to see would be right for Thomas as well as for her.

She turned towards him, took a deep breath and hoped her voice wouldn't shake as she demanded some answers.

'Just what exactly are you saying, Gib? Is this to do with the pretend kiss? Are you afraid I might have read something into what happened there on the plane and am now going to mark you down as my future Mr Right? As if you haven't made it perfectly clear that you're still in love with your wife! I mean, if a woman can't get the point from the wedding ring you're still wearing four years after her death, she'd have to be pretty dim. The woman, I mean.'

She saw Gib move, lifting his hand off the steering-wheel, but she was on a roll and not going to be deflected by a raised hand.

'Anyway, in case you're worried about any predatory instincts I might have, let me assure you that a man is the last thing I need in my life at the moment. My one and only concern right now is Thomas, and his security, well-being and happiness.'

She'd have added 'So, there' but was aware she was already sounding like a snooty adolescent so bit it back, fumbling for the door release so she could get out of the car and put distance between herself and this man and the way he made her feel.

'I took off the ring,' he said, voice as mild as milk. Then he slid his arm across her shoulders and drew her towards him. 'But that doesn't mean I'm ready for a permanent involvement in my life. What I said—about you living here—was more to do with me than with you. If you had another man in your life, maybe I'd stop wanting to kiss you. Stop wanting to hold you like this and tangle my hands in your hair and press my lips against yours, sinking into your sweet softness.'

He had drawn her so close she could feel the words puffing against her skin, as potent as caresses, warming her body with a wanting she'd never felt before.

'Are you going to stop talking and kiss me?' she asked, her throat so tight the words barely made it out. 'Or is this more pretend?'

'I can't pretend with you,' he said, so harshly she should have drawn away, but instead the roughness excited her even more and she gave in to the hot fire of his lips against hers and the heated dance of their tongues.

'Thanks a bunch,' Albert greeted Sophie when she walked into the ICU after not nearly enough sleep. 'Three more babies, one needing watching to make sure his heart keeps beating.'

'Anything to stop you being bored,' Sophie told him. 'Have the parents arrived yet?'

Albert smiled at her.

'Not yet, although I could probably tell you exactly where they are on the road. Helen, the mum, phones every ten minutes to see how the babies are doing.'

'I think being separated from your babies almost as soon as they are born must be the worst possible thing,' Sophie said, crossing to where the three were snuggled together in their crib and looking down at them. 'Content—they look content, don't they? Not worried, like so many of our babies look.'

'Do you think they somehow know they've hit the world too early, that they have that worried look?' Albert said, joining her beside the crib. 'With these three, all in together, they mightn't have realised yet that things have changed.'

'A more nonsensical conversation I have yet to hear.'

Sophie turned to the source of the remark, and found Gib had been smiling as he'd made it. Heat flashed through her as memories of the previous evening's kisses scorched her lips and set her heart racing, although the way they'd parted after it—silently, each to their own door—had left her as confused as she'd been shaken.

But Gib was smiling, and she smiled bravely back, then heard Albert whistle under his breath.

Annoyed with herself for revealing even a hint of her feelings, she moved away, heading for Mackenzie's crib, pausing to talk to Maria before she checked the monitors and read through the details of Mackenzie's night.

'She's doing OK, isn't she,' Maria said, making it more a statement than a question.

'Very OK at the moment,' Sophie agreed, seeing the latest measurement of the baby's tummy and realising it hadn't changed for thirty-six hours.

'So can I start giving her breast milk again?' Maria asked. 'When she was born, everyone said that was best, and now she's not getting it. What about all the things it's supposed to help, like her immunity and stuff?'

'It will still help when she gets back on it. I'll talk to Gib and see what he thinks. When we start to feed her again, it will have to be a tiny amount, then we'll gradually increase it.'

'That means my milk will keep going into the freezer,' Maria said, shaking her head as if that was a disaster.

'It keeps well that way,' Sophie assured her.

'But it loses the immunity stuff. I read that in the papers you gave us.'

Some days there was too much information and other days not enough, Sophie thought, though she hastened to assure Maria that the frozen milk would be kept for emergencies and Mackenzie would be given fresh milk as soon as her intestine was able to tolerate food.

'Dr Fisher to A and E. Dr Fisher to A and E.'

The call was so unexpected it took Sophie a moment to register she was Dr Fisher, then a squeezing of her heart—had Thomas had an accident?—before she remembered she was on call for emergencies this week.

'Trauma room two.' The triage nurse directed her to where she was needed, into a room already packed with people fighting to keep alive the victim of a road accident.

'You the neonatologist?' a man barked at her, and Sophie nodded.

'Hang around. She's pregnant but we've not had time to measure fundal height so don't know how far along, but we may have to take the baby. Scans show the foetus is all right. The woman suffered severe head injuries but little damage to the rest of her body. You'll be ready if we need you?'

Again Sophie nodded, having seen the emergency humidicrib outside the door of the room.

'We're losing her,' someone yelled, and Sophie was forgotten as the team fought to save the woman's life, people yelling orders, while one man pumped her chest, counting all the time, keeping blood flowing through the woman's body—through the placenta to her unborn child.

'It's no good. Look at the monitor—no brain activity at all.'

'But we've got foetal heartbeat. Keep the oxygen going, keep her heart pumping for the baby. Where's that damn obstetrician?'

'You called?'

A small woman clad in pale blue scrubs far too big for her pushed into the throng.

'I was delivering twins when the call came—newborn babies aren't the kind of things you can drop immediately.'

Chuckles from the tense staff told Sophie the ER staff knew and liked this woman, who was now bent over the accident victim, examining her only slightly swollen belly.

'I doubt she's more than thirty weeks,' she said at last, looking anxiously at the monitor, then at the head of the trauma team. 'You've called someone down from the NICU?'

He nodded towards Sophie, and the woman turned towards her.

'I'm Marty Cox. You heard. What do you think?'

Sophie didn't hesitate.

'That baby's going to have difficulties enough starting life without a mother, let alone all the potential hazards of being born ten weeks premature. Every day makes a difference at this stage. Can you keep her on life support—even for a week or two?'

'Keep her on it for six weeks and the baby has an even better chance,' Marty agreed.

'Whose permission do we need?' Sophie asked.

'Maybe not permission, but we'd need the husband's agreement, surely,' Marty told her.

'And the hospital ethics committee will want to know about it,' the ER doctor said. 'And the director of the ICU—he's the one who'll have to look after her so he's the one who should talk to her family. It will have to be in consultation with them. Then there's the cost...'

Marty rolled her eyes in Sophie's direction, checked that the ICU knew there was a problem, then promised to see someone from the ethics committee immediately.

'They usually get involved when it comes to turning off life support, but in the absence of family, surely they can make an interim decision,' Marty said, then added, 'You'd better come with me,' to Sophie, as the trauma team hooked their patient to full life support. 'Your knowledge of the chances of the little one's survival will carry more weight.'

'But what if the father opts not to go this way?' Sophie asked, after introducing herself to Marty.

'I would think someone will suggest counselling to help him make the decision—there'll be plenty of people only too willing to talk to him.'

She grinned at Sophie.

'Most times, the administrative palaver that goes on in this or in any big hospital drives me to distraction, but in cases like this they can chat to themselves all they like—it's giving our baby a better chance.'

'Our baby! I like that,' Sophie said, and Marty smiled again.

'Well, it is ours, isn't it? Mine until it's safely out, yours thereafter. Here's hoping the thereafter is at least another month away.'

She led Sophie into a lift, then pressed the button for the top floor.

'The bigwigs all lord it over us from up here. Have you met the medical director?'

'I met a lot of people the day of the interview. He might have been among them, but I can't remember.'

'Like the job?' Marty asked, and though Sophie was surprised, not so much by the question but by the fact she hadn't thought about it, she found herself answering with enthusiasm.

'I love it!'

Marty threw her a sideways glance as they got out of the lift, then raised her eyebrows.

'Haven't fallen in love with the boss, I hope,' she said. 'From all accounts, he's a lost cause.'

'I've only been here a week,' Sophie protested.

'Which isn't really answering my question,' Marty teased, then she led Sophie into a room furnished with a couch and a couple of comfortable-looking armchairs on one side, while on the other a very efficient-looking woman sat behind a pale timber desk, the top of which was so tidy Sophie automatically straightened her white coat.

'Kate, this is Sophie Fisher, the new neonatologist on Gib's team. Sophie, Kate Hall, keeper of the gate. Is the boss in?'

'He is, but you know he hates people barging in without an appointment,' Kate said.

'And I hate pregnant women dying in car accidents, especially ones with a viable foetus still inside them.'

'Oh, hell,' Kate muttered, and pressed a button on the large phone precisely set on the right-hand side of her tidy desk. She spoke swiftly but quietly and then obeyed some unheard command, saying, 'Go right in,' to Marty and Sophie.

'No baby?'

Gib spoke quietly as he saw Sophie come out of the lift outside the NICU. He knew she'd been called to an emergency, and returning without a baby meant only one thing.

'Not yet,' she said, sounding so tense he put his arm around her waist and guided her towards his office, not releasing her until she sank into a chair.

'Coffee?'

Anxious grey eyes lifted to meet his.

'Please,' she said quietly, then she dropped her head into her hands and he watched her shoulders move as she dragged in deep breaths. His heart hurt as he watched her, though he knew he had to remain professionally detached. What really bothered him was how he'd got to hurting-heart stage so quickly and with so little encouragement.

Could he put it down to lack of practice in relationships over the last four years?

Was it just a glitch?

He made two cups of coffee, thankful as ever for his espresso machine—a gift from the grateful family of one of his patients—then set them both on the small table in front of her and settled in the chair beside her, careful not to touch her lest the fire that burned between them flared again from last night's embers.

'The baby died?' he prompted.

She shook her head, breathed deeply again then raised her head, reached for her coffee and sipped it as she turned towards him.

'And I don't know if it's better or worse than that,' she muttered, her lovely eyes darkening with anxiety too deep to voice.

'Can anything be worse?' he said softly, wanting so badly to take her in his arms he had to hold onto the chair arms in case his hands disobeyed the orders of his brain.

'That's what I don't know,' she said helplessly, setting down her coffee cup and shaking her head at her uncertainty.

To hell with brain orders! Gib shifted to the arm of her chair and put his arm around her shoulders, drawing her close to his body, so her head rested against his chest. He stroked the shiny, smoothed-back hair with one hand and rubbed the other up and down her arm, all the time holding her close, feeling the movement of her chest as she breathed—the beating of her heart beneath her ribs.

This wasn't how he ached to hold her, but it was close— so close he gave in to the ache and used the hand that had stroked her hair to tilt her head towards him. Her eyes met his but they were unreadable, not forbidding him to do what he was about to do or daring him—nor asking.

He bent and kissed her lips, gently at first then with increasing pressure as he felt them move beneath his tender assault, responding...

This was wrong.

She needed—deserved—the best, and the best would be someone who was good at relationships.

He'd been tested in that department and had failed...

But she was kissing him back, her sweet taste seeping into him, her warmth stealing his resolve.

She moved first, pressing a hand against his chest to ease him back—away from her. She straightened up, ran her hands over her hair then sat back in the chair, dazed eyes meeting his, then focussing—angry.

'We're at work, Gib,' she reminded him. 'This personal nonsense between us, whatever it is, has no place here.'

'Is it nonsense?' he asked, although that wasn't the point at all.

She sighed and shook her head.

'I don't know,' she murmured helplessly.

He reached for her again, but this time contented himself with taking her hand.

'You're right, and I won't do that again, but physical comfort, touching, is sometimes all we can offer a person in need. A touch, a hug, a friendly kiss.'

'A friendly kiss?'

Dark eyebrows rose, then she shook her head again, straightened in her chair, retrieved her cup of coffee and sipped at the dregs.

Distancing herself from him, moving back to where she'd been before the kiss, she told him about the woman brought into A and E.

'Is it the first time you've come across this situation?'

She nodded again, then looked up at him.

'I know it's been done—in fact, I was the one who suggested it—but I've no idea what I think about it, Gib,' she admitted helplessly. 'Oh, I know it isn't up to me—it's up to the woman's husband, or her family, or to the hospital ethics committee or whoever, but I'm involved so how can I not know what to think about it?'

Gib touched her lightly on the shoulder.

'Hey, we've all been there,' he said gently, wanting to hold her again but knowing he'd already overstepped the line of professional behaviour. 'And to tell you the honest truth, I still have not so much doubts as uncertainties about it. We do know for a fact that keeping the mother on life support will give that baby a far better chance of a normal life—if there's any such thing as a normal life. But as far as the moral or ethical issues are concerned—what we think doesn't count, Sophie. As doctors, we have to be guided by those who know and love the woman. They will make a decision based on what she would want for her baby.'

'Do any of us know another person that well?' Sophie asked, lifting her head to study the man who was helping her through this maze—the man she realised she loved, and who kissed her with a burning passion she'd never experienced, but who couldn't offer her anything more.

'Did you know your wife well enough that you can say with absolute certainty she drove into that truck? It didn't sound that way when you told me of her death and yet you blame yourself.'

She touched his finger where the white indentation still marked the place his wedding ring had been. Then she looked into his blue eyes and saw the pain her question had caused.

Cursed herself, then tried to make amends.

'Gib, I have a theory about mental illness. I think too often people, non-psychiatrists, fail to remember all the time that it *is* an illness. Consider cancer, where sometimes treatment works and sometimes it doesn't. When it doesn't, the patient dies, no matter what we do to try to help them. But although various treatments work for the majority of people with mental illness, there are still a percentage where everything fails and death becomes inevitable.'

Standing up, she kissed him on the cheek.

'Stop blaming yourself,' she said quietly, then she left the room.

CHAPTER SEVEN

'CARLY, Kristie and Angus all have rising bilirubin levels—do you want to start them on phototherapy?'

'Oh, come on!' Sophie protested. 'It's Tuesday. My stars said I was going to have a really good Tuesday, and now you're telling me this when I've barely walked in the door!'

The nurse monitoring the three babies smiled at Sophie's grumble, and Sophie smiled back, not so much a return smile but at the use of all three of the babies' names. The triplets' parents had barely arrived from the country but already all the staff were calling their charges by their individual names.

Sophie studied the values on the test results and, although the levels weren't particularly high, opted to start treatment immediately.

'Is the phototherapy blanket in use?'

'Baby Neilsen is on it.'

Again Sophie smiled. Baby Neilsen's parents argued all day every day over what name to call their son, who was now five days old.

'Not getting any closer to a decision?' Sophie asked, and the nurse chuckled.

'It was Michael John last night, then Bradley John by breakfast time.'

'If the John part is decided, couldn't they just call him John?'

'No way, because it's the paternal grandfather's name, so it has to come second and the next baby, if they're not divorced before this one leaves hospital, will have her father's name second.'

Sophie sighed. It was a good thing Baby Neilsen was relatively healthy, because his parents were definitely more involved with their squabble than they were with him. Although the fact that all the unit knew about the goings-on was a sign that family involvement with the neonates was working well—the environment for the babies was as 'normal' as it was possible within such a high-care, high-tech setting.

'Use the phototherapy light for the—' She caught herself just in time. 'For Carly and Kristie and Angus. One at a time, starting with…' Sophie checked the test results again '…Kristie. Cover her eyes and her genitals, use protection yourself, and turn her regularly.'

Sophie caught the long-suffering look on the nurse's face and smiled at her.

'Teaching my grandmother to suck eggs—I know—but if I don't say these things every single time, the day might come when it's some new nurse who doesn't know the procedure. So I'll finish my spiel with a reminder that it causes dehydration so make sure she gets plenty of fluids. If Helen wants to nurse her some of the time, it would be good, but make sure she wears sunglasses and a cap. I'll check Baby Neilsen—we might be able to take him off the blanket later today—and get the secretary to check with Maintenance about the second light. Albert said it should be back this week. It would be good if we could get all three started on some treatment today.'

'I looked for you last night.'

Sophie didn't need to turn around to know it was Gib who'd murmured the words.

'Thomas and I went out,' she said, shuffling the triplets' test results in her hands as if the order of the pieces of paper was of prime importance.

'I did realise that,' Gib said gravely, his eyes catching her gaze—holding it for a moment before she slid her attention back to the papers in her hand.

'Did you hear the decision on your pregnant woman?'

Sophie nodded, having learned the woman was on life support in the ICU, although she still wasn't sure how she should feel about the situation.

'I'm happy for the baby,' she said.

'But you're still doubtful?'

He spoke so gently she looked up at him again, offering a lopsided smile.

'Pathetic, isn't it? A grown woman—trained doctor—and I don't know what I think about a particular situation.'

'It's not a situation the average grown woman—or even a trained doctor—has to consider very often,' he reminded her. 'Yet we face a similar dilemma time and time again, don't we, with babies born too soon?'

Sophie smiled at him, her face lighting up in the way he loved, seeming to shed radiance around her.

'I have no problems at all with that one,' she assured him. 'In a perfect world, all our babies would survive, but that's never going to happen. So I'll do my best to help every one of them, regardless of how fragile or immature they are. But it's funny, isn't it, how some babies are fighters? Even the smallest and sickliest can be born with a determination to live, and you seem to know right from the beginning—seem able to recognise the ones who'll never give up.'

'And the ones who choose to die,' Gib said quietly, and although Sophie knew that happened—that some preemies just didn't have the will to live and no amount of help could save them—she wondered if he was talking about babies.

Or about his wife?

'We should have the second phototherapy lamp back within an hour, so who do you want started next?'

The nurse had returned, ending both the conversation and Sophie's speculation. She refocussed on work.

'Carly next, but with you taking Kristie, we'll need another nurse to watch Carly, and also someone to keep an eye on Angus when he's left on his own. He doesn't like being parted from his sisters.'

'I'll tell Albert to organise it,' the nurse said, hurrying away.

Sophie turned to find Gib was over by Mackenzie's crib and slowly released the breath she'd been holding. Thankful to avoid a continuation of what had turned into a strange conversation, she crossed the unit in the other direction, anxious to explain to Helen and Dan what they intended doing to Carly, Kristie and Angus, and why.

But avoiding a colleague who worked in the same unit was impossible.

'Join me for lunch—we can talk about who's coming in to the follow-up clinic this afternoon.'

Gib caught up with her as she headed for the lifts.

Yesterday he'd kissed her. And the night before! Was he serious about a working lunch or should she read something more into the invitation?

She was so uncertain where she stood with Gib—uncertain even of where she wanted to stand—she sought refuge in a lie, not even crossing her fingers behind her back.

'I'm sorry, I'm meeting someone, but Marilyn gave me the files and I didn't see any problems with any of the patients she's allocated to me.'

He didn't answer for a moment, then he said, 'What about tonight? Would you trust Etty to babysit and have dinner with me?'

No work excuse!

Sophie's heart began to race so hard she had to press her hand against her chest to still it.

Had he changed his mind about involvement?

Did she want to get involved?

Were bananas yellow?

There's Thomas…

He likes Thomas…

Then she remembered.

'I'm sorry. I can't tonight. I'm seeing someone.'

He turned away before she could explain—could tell him the silly phrase she'd used didn't mean she was seeing someone romantically, but that her dinner date was with friends of Hilary's, to talk about the memorial service.

She swallowed hard and ducked through the nearest door, which, thankfully, once she'd looked around, was a women's restroom.

'Oh, Hilly, I do miss you,' she murmured, pressing her head against the cool mirror. 'Is it because I'm thinking of you so much this week that I'm such an emotional mess?'

'Talking to yourself?'

Marty Cox emerged from one of the cubicles.

'Worse,' Sophie told her. 'Talking to my dead sister.'

'Oh, I don't think that's worse,' Marty said, washing her hands then flicking water at Sophie. 'I think that's quite sensible. Although my half-sisters are so ratty that even if they were dead I'd hesitate to take their advice.'

Sophie had to laugh, then she washed her hands and splashed more water on her face, drying it on a paper towel.

'I'm on my way to lunch. Are you off? Want to join me?'

'I'd be delighted,' Sophie said, pleased she'd been able to remedy her lie but even more pleased to have the opportunity to talk to Marty, whose down-to-earth attitude might help her sort out her thoughts about the woman on life support and her unborn child.

Then she'd only have to sort out her thoughts about Gib and she'd be OK!

'How did your sister die?' Marty asked, when they'd chosen what they wanted for lunch and carried their trays to a corner of the canteen.

'Breast cancer.'

'Does it worry you—the familial thing?'

Sophie shook her head.

'I had genetic testing and I don't appear to have a problem. In fact, there's always been so much else to worry about since Hilary was diagnosed, apart from the testing which I had done at the hospital where I worked in Sydney, I haven't given it a thought.'

'But you check yourself?' Marty demanded, and Sophie wondered guiltily how long it had been since she had.

'Not often enough,' Marty surmised. 'Get your act into gear and do it regularly.'

'I will,' Sophie promised, then changed the subject, asking Marty about the woman through whom they'd met.

'She's my obstetrics patient now. As I'm on staff here, her obstetrician suggested I look after her. It's mainly a question of balancing her nutritional needs with regard to the pregnancy and checking on the foetus. The ICU staff see to her physical welfare, moving her limbs, turning her body, watching the monitors for any changes.'

'Does it worry you?' Sophie hadn't intended asking, but somehow the question popped out.

'Enormously,' Marty said. 'So much so I've become quite dotty. I touch her tummy and talk to the baby—the ICU staff think I'm mad—but the baby deserves more than to just *be* there, and if the family think this is what she'd have wanted, then surely she'd have wanted someone to keep talking to her child. Mind you, they're not ever there themselves. The bloke who was driving the car wasn't the husband, who's working somewhere overseas and hasn't been able to get back. Or maybe they couldn't contact him. Her parents made the decision about the baby. I'm not sure who the driver chap is, but he's just out of the ICU himself and is so distraught about her condition he can't cope with visiting her. I know people visit him, but not her, for some reason.'

'Because it's too darned hard,' Sophie said. 'It'd kill me if she was my sister. At least Hilary died peacefully at the end. But you're right about the baby. I'll come and talk to it, too. Do I need permission to go in?'

Marty smiled at her.

'I'll let them know you'll be up. Explain the baby's your province. It'll be a great treat for them to have two nutcases visiting the unit!'

Sophie laughed, grateful to Marty for cheering her up, not to mention diverting her thoughts, which had been veering dangerously close to self-pity.

Gib ordered sandwiches and ate them in his office, telling himself it was really good that Sophie hadn't wanted to have lunch with him—or dinner, for that matter. He wasn't sure why he'd asked her, given that he didn't want to get involved.

Was it wearing off—his commitment to non-involvement?

Or had a young woman with long black hair and smoky grey eyes bewitched him?

He should never have kissed her once, let alone three times.

'Yes!'

The loud jangle interrupted the thoughts he shouldn't be having, so he barked the word into the phone, then had to apologise to Claudia when he realised who it was.

'I just wanted to let you know there's a memorial service for Hilary Cooper this Friday at four.'

She gave him the address of a small non-denominational chapel where it was to be held, but although he jotted it down, he was barely listening—just waiting until she stopped talking so he could ask questions.

'So I thought you mightn't have heard and gave you a call,' she finished.

'Hilary's dead?'

'Oh, dear, you *didn't* know! Breast cancer nearly a year ago, poor thing.' The sympathy in Claudia's voice was only partly genuine—she and Hilary had never been close. 'You knew she'd gone back to Sydney—yes, of course you did, that was before you left. Well, apparently it was diagnosed soon after her return. She had treatment, of

course, but it was too aggressive and she lived—what?—
I suppose it would only be three years. Anyway, I thought
you'd want to know.'

And it was a good excuse to get in touch, Gib thought.
When he'd first joined the research institute Claudia had
made it obvious she was interested in him, and even inti-
mated that him being married wouldn't bother her.

'Thanks, Claudia. I'll certainly try to make it.'

'And I'll look forward to seeing you,' she said sweetly.

Gib hung up the phone then stared at it for a long time,
thoughts jostling senselessly in his head.

Hilary was dead. He'd liked Hilary—admired her self-
containment, her dedication to her job and her determination to get things right. That determination would have got
her through her initial treatment—in fact, she'd have
fought to the end.

But!

He rested one elbow on his desk and sank his forehead
into his palm, fingers scratching at his scalp as he tried to
make his mind work through the maze of conjecture
swirling in his head.

Had she been pregnant? The hormonal changes of pregnancy could trigger breast cancer in younger women, and
could hasten the grip it had on the patient.

She'd *wanted* a child, he reminded himself before more
guilt could sneak under his guard.

But had she had the child?

Had she even conceived?

He had no idea, but going to her memorial service
shifted from something he wanted to do for her to an opportunity to find out more.

Which made him feel guilty again!

'You do know you've got an outpatients' session?'

Marilyn had tapped on the door, before putting her head around the corner of it.

'Coming right now,' he told her, wondering just how long he'd sat with his head on his hand, useless conjecture clogging up his mind.

'Are you not well?'

Gib forced himself to smile at Mrs Jackson as he assured her he was fine.

'You seem distracted,' she persisted, although he was certain he'd explained quite lucidly that premature babies often had problems with their teeth.

'I'm sorry,' he said, taking another look at the baby teeth in Ellie's tiny mouth. 'We know that stress and illness can cause delay in teeth formation and also alter normal formation. It's during the last months of pregnancy that the enamel for teeth is put down—formed by calcium and phosphorus—so with preemies they might not have enough of these minerals stored for when their teeth come through. But usually only the baby teeth will be affected. Although Ellie's teeth now are grey and a bit pitted, her second teeth should be OK.'

Gib patted her on the head and Ellie took herself off to the corner of the room, where she pulled a puzzle off the shelf and sat at a small table to play with it.

'And if they're not?'

'Well, the most likely to be affected would be the first ones to come through, which are her front incisors and her six-year-old molars. A good paediatric dentist will be able to tell you more, and also help you teach Ellie how to care for her teeth.'

'Will she need braces?'

Gib smiled at Mrs Jackson.

'It's not only parents of preemies that ask that question about their children's teeth. I think every parent dreads the day when they have to include braces in their yearly budgets. I can't answer the question, and I doubt a dentist could either, until the new teeth come through, although X-rays could give some indication. But I'm sure if braces are the only problem she has in her future, we'll all be more than happy.'

Mrs Jackson laughed.

'You're right, but maybe I'm worrying about braces to stop myself worrying about other things. She starts school next year—it's so close now, and I'm terrified. Terrified I'll be a wimp about letting her go, terrified she'll find it too hard, terrified the other kids might tease her.'

'They're normal fears,' Gib said gently, 'but she's not going off alone. You've done everything you can to make the transition easy for her—she has friends from preschool going with her and she's a very sociable little being so I doubt anyone will laugh at her. It's more likely they'll treat her as special because she is so tiny.' He paused thoughtfully. 'Developmentally, well, as you know, we can't tell what learning difficulties she might have, but she coped so well at kindergarten and preschool. Look at her now, she's doing that reading readiness puzzle with no problems at all. I think she'll be fine, and if she has problems, well, she couldn't have two better or more supportive parents to give her extra help.'

'You're so good!' Mrs Jackson told him, bringing out a handkerchief and blowing her nose. 'Thanks, Gib.'

She tucked the handkerchief away then added, 'I suppose

you know that most of us parents come to see you for reassurance, rather than concerns over our preemies' health.'

'I sometimes wondered,' Gib said, standing up as she rose and coming to put an arm around her shoulders. 'Come whenever you like,' he assured her, as Ellie ran to take her mother's hand and the pair prepared to leave.

'Give Gib his present,' Mrs Jackson reminded her daughter, who opened up her shiny pink handbag and produced a small, clumsily wrapped parcel which Gib knew from experience would be aftershave lotion.

'Thank you,' he said, and meant it as he took the gift. Surely it didn't matter whether Hilary had had a child when he had all these surrogate children in his life?

He worked through the afternoon, collecting gifts as he did so, realising, when the last patient had departed and he was staring at the small pile, that he had still to buy presents for his family.

And on Saturday he was committed to helping Thomas decorate the tree.

Sunday, he could shop on Sunday. Mum and Dad, Aunt Etty, the Pritchards and Marilyn. Thank heavens for the magazine subscriptions he gave his sisters and their progeny! But the rest of the list was still there in the backwaters of his mind. And should he add Thomas? Surely he should. After all, Christmas was for kids and he was growing very fond of the little boy who shared his house.

Pity he was too young for aftershave!

'I think all of these are for you.'

Sophie came into his room and dropped another pile of presents on his desk.

'Thanks!' he said, and she chuckled at the dryness in his voice.

But seeing the presents, thinking of Thomas, he found himself wondering…

'What are you doing for Christmas?'

She looked startled, as if the presents, and the decorations going up both in the hospital and around his house, hadn't registered with her.

'I hadn't really thought about it,' she said. 'I'm happy to work if you want me to. Thomas is still too young to really understand what it's all about, and he certainly wouldn't know which day it was on, so he can open his presents any day I happen to have off, and we can take a picnic to the park, or whatever.'

'You don't have friends you're going to? No family up here?'

It wasn't that he was crazy about Christmas, feeling that the hype of it was overdone, but he usually called in to see Gillian's parents in the morning, on his way to lunch at his parents' place—a chaotic affair with sisters, nieces and nephews and, these days, boyfriends and girlfriends of the older ones.

So Sophie's quiet 'No' disturbed him, then he remembered her offer to work on a day staff hated working, and seized on it.

'If you really don't mind working…' he said tentatively.

'I don't,' she assured him. 'I'm happy to work Christmas Day, then Thomas and I will have our Christmas on Boxing Day.'

Although she sounded quite cheerful about the prospect, it seemed bleak to Gib, but before he could think of anything to say she'd left the room. No doubt to get ready for the 'someone' she was seeing.

He put the uneasiness in his stomach down to not finishing his sandwiches at lunchtime then remembered why he hadn't finished them and shook his head. Too many unconnected thoughts rampaging through his mind—he'd go home, have a swim…

And what?

Phone Claudia?

She'd be only too happy to have dinner with him.

Hell! Staying home watching something really dreary on television would be preferable.

He'd go home, have a swim and think about the rest later.

'Great,' Etty greeted him. 'Just the man I need. I've got to get my Christmas shortbread into the oven and Thomas is ready for his bedtime story. Would you mind?'

'Putting the shortbread into the oven? Not at all!'

'Reading to Thomas! Go!'

He went, although he felt like an intruder as he walked into the flat.

It was curiously impersonal. Apart from toys scattered around, there was little to suggest the place was tenanted.

Until he entered Thomas's room and saw the bright posters on the walls and the soft toys on the cabinet. More toys poked out of a wicker toybox at the bottom of his bed.

'Gib!' Delight lit the small face. 'Are you going to read my story?'

'I am,' he said, settling onto the side of the bed next to the little boy and taking the picture book from his hands. 'What's the story about?'

'An elephant,' Thomas told him. 'I like elephants.'

Thomas turned and pulled a tattered grey amorphous blob that might once have been an elephant into his arms, and smiled expectantly at Gib. But though the words 'I like elephants' were echoing through Gib's head, his eyes were riveted to a photo on the bedside table—previously hidden by the elephant—and his voice box seized up as his mind made leaps too confusing for rational thought to follow.

'Who is that in the photo?' he managed at last, and Thomas turned to touch the smiling face with his fingers.

'That's my mum,' he said, then he turned back to Gib. 'I don't really remember her, except that she was sick. Sophie said she really, really loved me, but mums are supposed to do that, aren't they? Can you read the story now?'

Could he read the story now?

How could he read?

How could he even sit here?

And Sophie?

Did she know?

Had she been keeping this a secret from him?

Or wasn't there a secret to keep?

'About the elephant?' Thomas prompted hopefully.

Gib opened the book and read the story, although his eyes kept straying to the child in the bed, and from the child to the photo of his mother—a laughing woman who had once asked Gib a favour...

A favour he'd at first refused...

Thomas fell asleep before the story finished, but Gib sat there, gazing at the sleeping boy, seeing the fair curls clustered around his face, seeing mental images of old photos of himself, with dark hair, not fair, but with curls.

Curls told you nothing. DNA—he could do a test! The idea that he was even considering taking a buccal swab from this child horrified him.

He closed the book, tucked the tatty elephant down

beside the sleeping child, then pulled the sheet up over both of them and bent to kiss the baby-soft cheek.

His mind barely working, he made his way back to the kitchen where Etty was taking trays of shortbread from the oven.

'Did you know Sophie isn't Thomas's mother?' he demanded, then, seeing Etty's quick frown, realised he'd probably spoken far too loudly.

'Not his biological mother, but my guess is she's the only mother he's really known. He showed me the picture of his mother and told me she'd died. From what I've gathered, she was Sophie's sister.'

But Hilary's name was Cooper, Gib's head protested, then he remembered talking to Hilary about marriage—heard her voice as clearly as if she was in the room.

'I'm not genetically programmed for marriage, Gib,' she'd said. 'My mother's on her third marriage, my father on his fourth. So it's definitely not in my plans.'

'And did you ask Sophie about her? About what happened to her?' he demanded of Etty.

Etty's frown returned.

'Why should I?'

Now Gib was frowning.

And growling.

'Natural curiosity, I would think!'

'Sophie's a very private person,' Etty said quietly. 'And I would never pry. I do know she's very stressed at the moment, in case you hadn't noticed. She's organising something for Friday. She started to tell me about it but Thomas fell over and scraped his knee and that was the end of that. She hasn't said anything to you?'

About organising a memorial service for her dead sister?

Of course she hadn't.

Why would she when he'd given her his spiel about non-involvement?

'We don't get much opportunity to chat,' he said, hoping he was concealing the irrational rage churning inside him.

'Maybe you should make some opportunities,' Etty said. 'Especially now you've taken off your wedding ring!'

Gib opened his mouth then closed it again but opened it once more to growl, 'I'm going for a swim.'

He whirled away, heading downstairs to the pool where he stripped off and plunged into the cool water, swimming laps with a ferocity that would, hopefully, leave him exhausted enough to sleep.

But swimming didn't take much brain power, and his mind tried to make sense of what he'd learned and debated the future—and the relevance of the past.

He'd said no at first—when Hilary had asked. No, and no, and no. He was married and wouldn't contemplate having a child outside his marriage, neither would he dream of being unfaithful, even at arm's length, to Gillian.

Then Gillian had died, and in his despair and grief and agony, in the muddle of his mind where fear that he had failed her had grown unchallenged, he'd changed his mind, thinking if he could bring some happiness into one woman's life, it might somehow, in part at least, make amends.

Hilary had been adamant she'd never make a claim on him—that the child would be hers and hers alone.

Tumble-turn and another lap.

And he'd promised Hilary he'd never make a claim on the child, never reveal his paternity or ask to be involved. Filled as he'd been with remorse and sadness over Gillian's death, that had been an easy promise to make. He'd not wanted or needed to be a father, and, anyway, he had children in his life—children he cared for and made well, then passed back to their parents. Not to mention nieces and nephews. That was enough, he'd told Hilary—and himself.

But in the emotional tumult of that time he'd somehow failed to think through that promise—he'd failed to consider the child.

How fair had they both been to him? To deny him a father—deny him all knowledge of his father?

Not fair at all…

But now Hilary was gone, things were different. With her death, the promise had to be broken.

He had to say something to Sophie—but how? When?

He turned and swam back the other way.

Sophie let herself into the door of the flat, aware of the silence in the big house, going first to Thomas's room where she smiled at the sleeping cherub before bending to kiss his cheek.

'Two more days, Thomas,' she whispered to him. 'Two more days then maybe we'll know something.'

She sat for a moment, looking at his face, seeking some definition in features that still held the chubby blandness of babyhood, and though her heart skipped a beat at the possibility of losing this precious child, she was beginning to think she had to find his father for his sake, as well as for hers.

One day he'd want to know! One day he'd become aware that other children had two parents.

How old would he be when that happened—when he started asking questions about his father?

And would she tell him what she knew, even if the man

stuck to his decision to have nothing to do with his child? Hilary had always said it had been she who'd insisted on this arrangement, but had she been protecting a man she loved?

Sophie suspected this was the case, not being able to imagine Hilary having an affair with someone she didn't love. But whatever had happened in the past, she needed this man now—needed his consent to her formal adoption of Thomas, needed him to keep Thomas safe...

CHAPTER EIGHT

BY FRIDAY Gib had rationalised most of his wild supposi-
tions. For a start, he'd decided that Hilary Cooper had kept
to their agreement—had stuck to her promise not to ever
reveal who had fathered her baby.

Sophie didn't have a clue.

Not that he could be certain Thomas *was* his child,
although he'd dug out the photo album his mother had pre-
sented to him on his twenty-first birthday and studied
numerous photos of his three-year-old self, trying to
compare the photos to the little boy.

The timing was right.

He worked through the day, missing Sophie's presence,
saddened that she was going through something as emo-
tionally distressing as preparing for a memorial service for
her sister yet hadn't told him.

Why should she?

At three-thirty he left the hospital, driving reluctantly
to the small chapel on a hill on the outskirts of the city, not
sure exactly why he was going to the service.

In memory of a friend, he told himself, although he
knew his original impulse to attend had been to find out
about a child—something he now knew. Or kind of knew!

As support for Sophie?

When she hadn't asked for support?

He shook aside useless speculation and concentrated on driving. The traffic was thicker than he'd expected, with inexplicable hold-ups every few hundred metres.

Sophie had finished what she had to say about Hilary, had handed over to Paula, Hilary's best friend at the institute, and was moving to take her seat in the front row when she saw him come in.

Gib?

Here?

Had someone told him she was doing this?

Had he come to offer his support to her?

Warmth crept through her body. For all his talk of non-involvement she'd felt they were getting closer. As well as the kisses, there'd been a touch here, a look there, and although this week she'd been too distracted to think much about it, there'd been his dinner invitation as well.

The last few days she'd seen less of him—he'd had a series of hospital meetings and had been away overnight last night—but now this was over and done with—

She pulled herself out of this pleasant but useless speculation, reminding herself of her purpose in holding the service. Yes, it was to honour Hilary, but it was more important was to check out who had attended.

What men attended!

There was a book to sign at the front of the chapel, and she'd asked people to put both their names and their addresses, but she squirmed in her seat, wanting to check out the male attendees, wondering which one her sister had loved.

Paula finished speaking, then invited everyone to stand

and sing, as it was Christmas, Hilary's favourite carol, and as the voices rose in the simple melody of 'Silent Night', Sophie forgot her quest, forgot her problems, even forgot Gib, thinking only of the sister who had protected and nurtured her all her life—the sister she had loved with all her heart.

The carol finished, people began to file out. She should be at the door with Paula, thanking them for coming, but tears Sophie couldn't stem were seeping from her eyes, and she sank back down onto the seat and wrapped her arms around her shoulders, hoping the storm would pass.

'Hey!'

It was Gib, there beside her, the gentle word spoken so he didn't startle her.

Now he put his arms around her and drew her close, pressing her head to his shoulder and holding her tight.

'Hey,' he said again. 'It's OK to cry, Sophie. Sometimes it's what we need to do to cleanse the grief.'

She snuggled closer in his arms, the tears subsiding, taking the handkerchief he handed her and scrubbing at her face—seeing make-up smear across it and knowing she couldn't give it back.

'Oh, dear, I'm sorry. You might not believe this, but I've never been a teary person. Now I seem to be making a habit of it—and, worse, a habit of needing comfort so you end up having to put your arms around me.'

'It's not exactly a hardship,' he murmured, running his hand down her arm, soothing and stroking until the feeling changed from solace to something else.

'Thank you for being here.' Sophie tried to straighten up, to move away from him, but he held her close. So she spoke instead, hoping words might distract her from the feeling his hand was generating 'It's been a year and I was sure I could manage. I had no idea I'd crack up like this.'

She should ask him how he'd known to come, but it was so nice, being held against his chest, she decided it didn't matter. Especially as his lips were pressing against her hair and if she moved her head just a little they'd meet skin.

Then another small shift in their configuration and lips could touch...

'Do you want to take the flowers?'

Sophie jerked away from Gib, unable to believe she was sitting in a chapel, kissing her boss, right after her sister's memorial service.

'Could you send them to the hospital?' she told the man as she struggled to her feet. Her knees were wobbly, her toes still tingling, but somehow she made it upright.

'What hospital?' the man was asking, and fortunately Gib took over, telling the man where to send the flowers then leading her gently out of the chapel.

'Let's leave your car. I can run you back to get it in the morning,' he suggested, and Sophie, given the uncertainty of her lower limbs, was happy to agree, although now, as she stared at the all but deserted car park, she started worrying about her behaviour.

'This is terrible! I should have talked to people—thanked them for coming—stood with Paula at the door...'

'People will understand,' Gib soothed, pleased they'd sat long enough for everyone—Claudia in particular—to have departed. 'And you've got the guest book.' He'd picked it up himself. 'You can write and thank people.'

Sophie nodded, happy to accept the excuses he was making on her behalf, happy just to be with him, to have his arm around her shoulders and the long length of his body pressed against her side.

He opened the car door for her, and held it while she got in, then, when he'd settled himself behind the wheel, he leant across and kissed her gently on the lips.

'I think a walk on the beach might be what we both need,' he said, and delight flooded through Sophie's body.

'The beach? Brisbane's got a beach?'

'No, but the Gold Coast has fifty kilometres of beaches and we're less than half an hour away.'

'I'll have to phone Etty.'

He handed her his mobile, but though her fingers shook with emotion—to walk with Gib on a beach at sunset? To touch? To kiss again?—she hesitated.

'I should go home,' she muttered. 'I know Thomas loves Etty but I do feel guilty if I leave him with her when it's not work-related.'

'Etty was going to pop corn and string it onto thread for the tree—do you really think Thomas will miss you with all that going on?'

He took the phone from her restless fingers and made the call himself, passing it back to her so she could talk to the little boy.

Gib had been right—Thomas was so excited about the popcorn she could barely get a word in.

'Etty's wonderful,' she said, as she slipped the phone into the console between them. 'I've never thanked you for finding her for me—or giving her to me might be more like it. And for the flat, which makes things so much easier.'

He was pulling out of the parking area and she turned and laid her hand gently on his cheek.

'Thank you for everything.'

He turned his head far enough to press a kiss against her palm and then kept his concentration on the road, a small frown on his face as he wove through the traffic.

Could he do it? Commit to another woman and not make the mistakes he'd made with Gillian? Was Sophie right about mental illness? That some deaths were inevitable?

Could he accept it and move on?

Marry Sophie?

It would be the perfect solution, Gib realised as he drove up the ramp onto the motorway. He'd have his son—he'd have Sophie. Muscles tightened at the thought.

'You look worried. Is it Mackenzie?'

He felt Sophie's hand touch his leg as she asked the question, and turned to see anxiety in her face.

'Not Mackenzie,' he assured her, wishing he could tell her of his chaotic thoughts, but he needed to wait at least until he'd sorted through the chaos and reached a rational decision that he knew for certain wasn't based on his increasingly irresistible attraction to the woman by his side.

She didn't probe, simply rested back in the seat and closed her eyes, her hand still creating a warm spot on his leg and sending wayward messages along his nerves.

'Beach!' he announced some time later, pulling up in the parking area at Narrowneck and smiling with delight as he saw the tide was low and the long, wide stretch of sand was virtually deserted.

He took off his shoes, rolled up his trousers and got out of the car, opening Sophie's door and waiting as she slipped off her sandals. Then he took her hand and led her down the boarded path that protected the dunes from too much wear and tear.

But once on the beach proper, he lost her, for she ran

ahead, long legs lifting high as she headed towards the water, then her skirt lifting to show even more leg as she splashed in the shallows.

'Oh, Gib,' she said, turning a radiant smile in his direction. 'This is so exactly what I needed.'

She threw her arms into the air as if to embrace the sky, sea and sand, then splashed again, kicking at the water so diamond drops of it sprayed through the air.

Behind them, the dying rays of the sun had turned the heavens pink, but already, on the far horizon, they could see the sky lightening as if the moon would soon be shedding its silvery light across the water.

He took her hand again, and together they walked through the little waves that ebbed and flowed around their feet.

Had he ever felt so at ease with Gillian?

He could remember excitement, could remember despair, but contentment?

Had he not been seeking it that it had eluded him?

Was it an age thing that suddenly it seemed so important—as if this was how he'd like to feel for ever?

'I should have gone home to Thomas.'

The guilt in Sophie's voice brought him out of his reverie. He knew all about guilt—knew how it could excoriate a person's soul.

'He was happy when we phoned,' he reminded Sophie, though he knew all the excuses in the world wouldn't ease the guilt. 'Don't you ever programme time just for Sophie?'

He stopped walking and used their clasped hands to tug her close.

'Not these days I don't,' she whispered. 'Since Hilary died, well, Thomas was only two, he needed a lot of my attention.'

Would she tell him now? Tell him Thomas was Hilary's son and so lead into a conversation he knew he had to have with her?

He waited, but she'd turned away, gazing out towards the far horizon, leaving him with a sense of disappointment that she didn't trust him enough to confide in him.

Was it fear that she'd lose the child she so obviously adored?

In which case, if she even so much as suspected he was Thomas's father, would she flee?

Cold dread inside him told him how he'd feel about *that* particular scenario!

He hadn't realised he'd sighed until she turned towards him and once more placed a hand against his cheek.

'This is Sophie time,' she said quietly, and he forgot everything but his attraction to this woman, the length of her body against his, the feel of silken hair sliding through his fingers. He eased his hands into the neat pleat of hair and found the pins that held it in place, pulling them out and hurling them into the ocean before combing his fingers through the dark tresses so they spread across her shoulders.

Then, in case she was thinking of explaining her statement, or fretting more about Thomas, he stopped her lips with a kiss, drawing her body towards him until it melded with his, feeling her soft breasts against his chest, drinking in the taste and scent of her—content!

Sophie felt his body pressed against hers, his hands making magic happen to her skin. His kiss teased and probed and plundered, filling her with a tingling excitement that went far beyond her toes.

Deep muscles that had been dormant for a long time tensed, and heat burned at the very centre of her being, and with the tingling and the heat and the heady happiness came a certainty that this was her man, so she kissed him back, losing herself in kisses—losing the sadness of the past and making promises to the future.

Well, she was, but was he?

'This is non-involvement?' she said lightly, easing away from him a long time later.

He pressed a final kiss to her lips then turned her to walk again on the wet sand.

'Look,' he said, and they stopped to watch the magic of the moon rise, red-gold and huge, out of the sea.

'I've been thinking about what you said,' he told her quietly, but that was all, and they walked again.

But Sophie's heart brimmed with happiness. Maybe, just maybe, the love she felt for Gib would eventually be returned.

They strolled for an hour, reaching a long jetty Gib explained was the sand-pumping jetty, pumping sand that clogged the narrow seaway far out into the waves where wave action helped it build up sand deposits on the beaches.

'There's a café up behind the dunes. Fancy some fish and chips?' he added.

'In paper? Can we eat them on the sand?'

He dropped a short, sweet kiss on her lips.

'We can,' he promised, then took her hand and led her up through the dunes.

So they ate fish and chips on the beach then washed their sticky fingers in the ocean, walked back to the car and drove home, not talking much, although it seemed to Sophie that contentment lay between them.

Thomas was still up, excited by the idea that his Christmas

tree was coming the very next day, so they had a night swim, the little boy again showing off for Gib, Sophie again wondering about the little show-off's father.

Surely having a father in his life would be a good thing. She and Hilary hadn't had much luck with fathers but that wasn't to say Thomas's father would be anything like either of them—although to have an affair with Hilary then say he wanted nothing to do with the child, that had been cold...

'Sophie, watch this!'

Thomas was on Gib's shoulders, squealing with delight as Gib's strong hands lifted him and threw him into the water—high enough to please Thomas with the dangerous adventure but gently enough for Sophie not to worry.

Gib would make a wonderful father.

The thought shocked her. How could she be thinking that far ahead on the basis of a few kisses—most of which, if she had to be perfectly honest, had come from kindness on Gib's part?

Even today...

'Watch, Sophie!'

She watched them both playing in the water and her heart hurt because it was all becoming so difficult.

On a practical point, she should say something about not getting Thomas too excited before he went to bed, but she knew swimming was the best thing to tire him out, and he'd splash around for a while then be happy to go to bed.

And Gib? What would he do when they finished swimming?

Suggest they go down and watch the river gliding by?

Continue the kissing they'd shared on the beach?

It was too early to take things further than that, she

warned her body, which had grown excited at the thought, little shock waves of desire rippling through it.

'Bedtime,' she said to Thomas, catching him in her arms as he swam towards her and giving him a hug. His chubby little arms wrapped around her and he returned her hug, nestling his head against her shoulder.

'I love you, Sophie,' he said. 'And I love Aunt Etty, and I love Gib.'

Sophie glanced towards Gib to see how he'd taken this declaration, and caught a strange expression in his eyes.

Or maybe his eyes looked perfectly normal and it was the subdued lighting from the pool that made them look...

Not sad, exactly.

She set Thomas on the edge of the pool and climbed out. Still embarrassed about displaying her body in front of Gib, she wrapped a towel quickly around her waist. She was drying Thomas when the pager buzzed, and though she automatically reached for the chair where hers would have been, it wasn't there.

'It's mine,' Gib told her, shaking water off his hands before picking up the small machine. 'The hospital. I'm on call so I guess they need me.'

He crossed to where a phone had been installed near a small cabana used for showering and changing, and Sophie watched him, seeing his long, lean, near-naked body, and her mouth dried with the hunger that attraction brought in its wake.

She diverted it by drying herself then lifting Thomas into her arms.

'Woman in labour, thirty-five weeks,' he said, putting down the phone and picking up his towel, drying himself with brisk efficiency. 'Pity,' he added, with a wry smile at Sophie.

Then he took two long strides towards them and planted a kiss on Thomas's cheek.

'Goodnight, little man,' he said, then he touched Sophie on the head.

'Goodnight to you, too,' he added, huskily enough for Sophie to know that they would probably have done more tonight than watch the river glide by…

Thomas woke with the dawn and it was all Sophie could do to keep him occupied until nine, when the man was due to arrive with the tree. She'd brought out all the old baubles she and Hilary had collected when they'd lived with their grandmother, but their trees had usually been small in size so the baubles had been adequate.

But on a huge tree?

'See what Aunt Etty and me did?' Thomas demanded when, at five to nine, Sophie decreed it was time to go through to the big sitting room.

He pointed at a bowl of strung popcorn and Sophie stopped worrying about having enough decorations. The popcorn would be enough to cover one of the Norfolk pines they'd seen at the beach the previous evening.

Etty greeted both of them with delight, then waved her hand towards a large box in one corner of the room.

'Gib's collected a lot of decorations over the years,' she said, then added, 'Some years Gillian was really into Christmas and some years she wasn't, but he still put up a tree and decorated the living room.'

More evidence that he *was* a nice man! Sophie thought, then wondered why 'nice' when such a basic, necessary, character trait had never featured before in her list of what she liked in men.

She was smiling to herself about it when the 'nice' man appeared, looking slightly rumpled as if he hadn't had enough sleep but was determined to do his duty with the tree.

'Good morning,' he said generally, and though Thomas went towards him, demanding he look at the popcorn he had threaded, it was to Sophie that Gib's gaze shifted.

'Everything go all right?' she asked, and he smiled and nodded.

'Biggest five-week premmie baby I've ever handled. We'll keep her a day or two, but she'll do extremely well. It was just a long labour so I'm a little short on sleep.'

'Go back to bed. We can manage the tree.'

'No way. I'm here to do the high bits, aren't I, Thomas?'

'Tree's here,' Etty said, looking out the kitchen window to where a truck was pulling into the yard.

And so began the best day Sophie could remember having had for a long, long time.

They talked and laughed and ate the Christmas goodies Etty kept providing. Thomas decorated the lower branches in a haphazard way that Sophie corrected where she could, then Gib lifted the little boy up to put his popcorn strings and colourful baubles higher up.

Could they be a family?

The thought kept sneaking into Sophie's head, no matter how hard she tried not to think it.

Be content for the happiness of today, she warned herself, but she knew she wanted more.

Wanted Gib.

Wanted to be a family!

Thomas was so worn out he slept most of the afternoon, Gib went back to the hospital to check the new arrival, and

Sophie reluctantly opened the visitors' book from the memorial service.

She would write to everyone who'd attended, thanking them for coming, but the eight men—she hadn't noticed that many—what would she do about them? Look up phone numbers and call them? Ask them straight out if they'd had an affair with her sister about four years ago?

Although she couldn't remember the precise details of the various conversations she was certain, from something Hilary had said, that Thomas's father had been a work colleague—but to phone and ask?

Impossible!

Suddenly the service that had seemed like such a good idea was revealed as a flop. No, the service hadn't been a flop—it had been her weak collapse at the end of it that had ruined the idea. Surely if she'd stood at the door and checked out the men, she might have been able to tell which one Hilary had loved.

How? None would have worn an 'I loved Hilary' stamp on their forehead.

In fact, though she had known Hilary well enough to know she wouldn't have had an affair without love, there was no guarantee that the man concerned had loved her back.

The most obvious supposition was that he was married— why else would he not have wanted to know about a child?

Sophie sighed. What to do with the list of names she'd so cleverly collected?

Paula might know, but she'd pestered Paula enough this week. Then let her down by not standing at the door with her after the service.

And asking Paula was bringing someone else into the

picture and making a muck of Hilary's promise not to reveal the information.

Was there any other way to find out who Hilary had been close to at the institute?

No!

She'd phone Paula tomorrow—putting it off because today was such a joyful day she didn't want to spoil it.

'Barbeque tonight so we can stand down on the lowest terrace and look back up at the brilliant lights on our brilliant tree,' Gib announced late that afternoon, when he'd finally found the errant bulb in the string of multicoloured lights and had replaced it so now all the lights were working.

'I'll help,' Thomas volunteered, so he and Gib departed to get the barbeque ready while Sophie followed Etty to the kitchen, determined to give the older woman a hand, although she never asked for help and was more likely to shoo Sophie away when she suggested helping.

'They get on well, Gib and Thomas,' Etty said, and although the words were carefully guileless, Sophie had to laugh.

'He says you've been trying to match him up to someone since his wife died,' she teased Etty, and though Etty smiled she shook her head.

'For a long time it was too soon, then there was his guilt over the way Gillian died. It wasn't his fault—he didn't drive her to it—in fact, no man could have been better to any woman, but she was sick and she was sick of being sick. She was angry with the illness, angry with Gib—angry with the world.'

'It's a terrible thing, mental illness,' Sophie said quietly, and Etty nodded her agreement.

'Far worse than spina bifida,' she said. 'Worse than anything, if you ask me.'

'Ask you what?'

Gib had returned, Thomas on his shoulders.

'Ask you what kind of meat you want. I've steak and sausages or some chicken I could marinate.'

'Sausages!' Thomas decided instantly, while Gib took a little longer to suggest that chicken might be nice for a change.

'And sausages?' Thomas said hopefully.

'We'll have both,' Etty assured him.

The menfolk then departed, but now the conversation turned to food—what to have with chicken and sausages.

So normal!

So nice!

But later, with Thomas tucked up in bed asleep and Etty working on her tapestry, the kisses Sophie shared with Gib went so far beyond nice—so far beyond anything she'd ever imagined—Sophie wondered if she needed a new dictionary.

They were by the river, in the shadows of the gazebo, and Gib's lips explored her skin with a hunger that made her tremble all over, her knees so weak she had to cling to him for support.

'You make it so hard for me to keep my resolve to not get involved,' he told her, punctuating the sentence with a kiss between each word. One to her ear, one on her neck, one on the corner of her eye, one for her nose—kisses brushing like the wings of butterflies across her face, kisses that seemed to promise the things he was finding it difficult to say.

They're just kisses, she tried to tell herself, but they felt like more.

They felt like involvement.

'There's a sun lounge by the pool—we'd be more comfortable lying down,' he murmured.

Drugged by kisses, it would have been easy to say yes, but caution told Sophie they were going too far, too fast. This was a man who only this week had taken off his wedding ring.

Four years after his wife had died!

A wife who'd brought magic into his life.

'Not yet,' she whispered against his lips, and held her breath while she waited for a reaction.

He tightened his grip on her, holding her so it seemed every bit of her was touching him.

'You are wise to be cautious,' he whispered. 'Cautious for both of us.'

Then he kissed her again and she could have cried with regret at her decision, for her body burned for him to take it so together they could share the bliss, the exquisite joy of satisfying sex—the ultimate release.

'Can I change my mind?' she asked, breaking away from him so she could breathe.

He laughed out loud—a joyous sound that suggested he was as happy as she was in this situation.

'Not tonight,' he told her. 'I think you meant it when you said not yet, and decisions are best not made at night. Think about it tomorrow—and the next day, too, because I've got to fly to Sydney for a meeting.'

He kissed her again, but gently this time, not stealing her breath and her resolve.

'But come Monday evening—Christmas Eve—with Thomas tucked up in bed early because Santa will be coming, then maybe we'll find some mistletoe above a bed somewhere, sweet Sophie, and you and I will share a very special Christmas.'

'Christmas Eve maybe,' Sophie told him, taking her turn to punctuate her words with kisses. 'But my dreadful boss has rostered me on duty Christmas Day so Thomas's and my Christmas will be delayed.'

'Oh, hell! I'd forgotten all about it. I can change it. Maybe Yui might want to work, or Rod—someone, anyone!'

He sounded so despairing Sophie laughed and hugged him tight. She'd have liked to say they'd have other Christmases—many of them—but the caution that had made her say not yet held her back from tempting fate with such a declaration.

Gib felt her withdrawal and wondered if she was regretting her decision to work on Christmas Day and so not spend it with Thomas.

Thomas. He should talk to her about Thomas.

Whenever his brain cells weren't bamboozled by the attraction he felt towards her, his mind pondered the problem that was Thomas. He swung one way then another, one minute determined to explain his suspicion to her, the next feeling uncertain of how to go about it. What if he was wrong? What if he was right? He couldn't just drop a bombshell like this—either way, there would be repercussions.

He *had* to figure it out! Maybe two days away from Sophie was what he needed—two days to clear his head and get his thinking straight. In the meantime, he could be practical.

'Etty usually comes with me to my family's place for Christmas lunch,' Gib said, his arms loosely around Sophie's waist because he couldn't yet let go of her completely. 'It's a bun fight, with my sisters and their kids and the odd aunt or two, but I think…'

Suddenly he felt hesitant, knowing he should sort out

the father-thing before Christmas Day—knowing he'd be overwhelmed with pride and happiness to introduce the little boy to his family as his son.

'Thomas would enjoy it,' Sophie finished for him. 'I'm sure he would, but we'd better ask Etty if she minds, because she'd have to be responsible for him. If she'd rather not, the child-care centre will be open. It has to be so the staff on duty have somewhere for their kids.'

'Etty won't mind,' he said, certain he was right, and certain also he could work out, over the next two days, how to talk to Sophie about his thoughts, so this Christmas would be special in more ways than one.

CHAPTER NINE

GIB all but bounced into the unit on Christmas Eve. He'd come straight from the airport and the one thing in his mind had been seeing Sophie again. He knew he wouldn't be able to grab her in a bear hug and swing her in the air and kiss her the way he wanted to kiss her, but just seeing her would keep him going.

Then later he'd order lunch for them and have it sent up to his office—something nice from the café, not damp, re-frigerated sandwiches. And he'd explain about himself and Hilary and tell her what he thought.

She'd be surprised, of course, but she'd also see just how ideal it all was—that he, she and Thomas could be a family…

'Where's Sophie?' he demanded when he'd checked her office and once again walked through the NICU in search of her.

The silence told him there was something wrong.

Very wrong.

In fact, Albert and Sally both looked ill.

'What's happened?' Gib demanded, certain if something bad had occurred Etty would have phoned him.

'There's a crisis at the child-care centre. Some man's gone in there with a knife and he's holding a little boy hostage.'

'Not Thomas!'

Gib heard the words roar from his throat, never heeding his own insistence that there should be no loud noises in the ICU. He dashed from the room, hit the lift button, then told himself to calm down—that pounding on the doors would do no good.

Sophie, white-faced with fear, stood with other equally desperate parents outside the centre. He pushed towards her and grabbed her shoulders, pulling her against his body for a hug before easing her back away and looking down into her face.

'What happened?' he demanded, his voice still way too loud.

'A man,' she said, fear making her usually deep voice thin and reedy. 'His child is dying in the children's ICU— apparently he backed over him in a car. Imagine how demented he must feel...'

'He could be holding Thomas hostage—you *can't* feel sorry for him!'

Grey eyes looked helplessly into his.

'Of course I do, but that's not the issue here.'

Gib calmed down slightly, knowing Sophie deserved his support, not his anger.

'What is?' he asked, as more police arrived, one with a loudhailer.

'The man's child won't live, and someone asked the man if he'd agree to donate his organs.'

'Hell! The man's just run over his son and killed him and some idiot asks if they can use the kid for spare parts.' Anger boiled within him once again, not placated by Sophie's quiet explanation.

'There's a baby in the cardiac ICU that desperately needs a heart.'

Gib swore again, unable to contain himself, then he listened while a policeman called to the man inside.

The loudhailer distorted the words, but the furious, heart-broken father needed no such aid to make himself heard.

'Get away, the lot of you. If you come in I'll kill this kid, and maybe more than one. That way, you'll have plenty of hearts to give away.'

'What's his boy's name?' Gib asked, and though Sophie knew she'd heard it, she couldn't bring it to mind.

'It's Michael,' another woman said. 'I'm a nurse in A and E. I was there when they brought him in.'

'I'm going in,' Gib said, and Sophie automatically moved in front of him, clinging to his arm, begging him to wait, but he pushed past, coming to the line of police who blocked off the gate.

'You can't go in, Gib,' Sophie said, following helplessly in his wake, her grasping hands futile against his strength. 'The police know what they're doing. They're trained for this kind of thing—we have to believe that.'

'She's right, sir,' the nearest policeman said, although he was young and not particularly strong-looking so Sophie doubted he'd stop a determined Gib. 'Our mediator will be here soon. He'll talk him out.'

'Or not!' Gib said bluntly. 'You don't know that's going to work, and in the meantime my son is being traumatised by a man with a knife. I'm going in.'

He pushed past the policeman, while Sophie, unable to stop him, stood, shocked into immobility by two words.

My son!

Maybe it was a figure of speech.

Maybe he was thinking ahead to a time when they might marry.

Maybe he was doing it for her.

Too many maybes, and in the meantime Gib had stormed into the centre, calling out to the man, telling him he was a doctor sent to get him because Michael was conscious and wanted to talk to him.

The woman beside Sophie gave a cry of fear, while the policeman muttered about not telling lies to hostage-takers, but Sophie could only think of Gib and Thomas…

Gib didn't know if it would work, but he hadn't been able to come up with anything else, and instinct suggested the man would react to news that his child was not yet dead.

He was right, for the man, a burly-looking thirty-something in footy shorts and a bright Hawaiian shirt, let go of the little boy he'd been holding, patted his shoulder and turned to Gib, the open penknife wavering in his hand.

'Come on, mate, I'll take you up,' Gib said, putting his arm around the man's shoulders and leading him out of the centre. 'Out of the way,' he ordered the police, holding tight to the man in case someone moved too suddenly or said something to freak him out again. 'Someone get a lift down for us. We're going straight upstairs.'

He was so intent on getting the man somewhere quiet so he could explain his lie, he barely noticed Sophie staring at him as if transfixed, white horror still etched on her face, although she must know by now that Thomas would be safe.

The police fell back and although someone suggested the man give up his knife, he clung to it, holding it still open but by his side.

Once in the lift, Gib pressed the button for the floor

they needed, then turned to the man and put his hands on his shoulders.

This was the moment when things could get nasty but he couldn't let the man continue to believe the lie. At least with just the two of them in the lift, he, Gib, was the only one who could get hurt.

'I lied to you, mate,' he said quietly. 'But I had to get you out of there. Hurting a child down there wasn't going to make things right for your Michael, and how would your wife have coped if you'd ended up in jail? Now, more than ever before, she needs you by her side. She needs you with her when she says goodbye to Michael, needs you to hold her, and needs you to share her grief.'

The man looked at him with stricken eyes.

'He's not alive?'

'Not really,' Gib said gently, aware this could be the moment when the man used the knife.

'But it's me that killed him. I backed over him. We were going to the beach—I was getting the car out—I thought he was with Lisa then there was a bump.'

Gib put his arms around the man and gave him a hug.

'She won't want to talk to me—she won't want me near her. Why would she?'

The words were broken by sobs and Gib stopped the lift between floors, a trick he'd learned while in med school, and held the man until the wild flood of grief had eased.

'It must be the very worst thing that can ever happen to a human being, but don't you think your wife will be blaming herself as well—blaming herself for not watching him? Neither of you are to blame—it was an accident. You can't carry that kind of guilt through your lives. These things happen and we can only suppose that for some reason they are meant to be.'

The man pushed away and folded up his knife, then held it in the palm of his hand and stared at it as if trying to work out what it was.

'We were going to go fishing. That's why I had the knife. It's got little tweezers on it for holding the fish hook while you tease it out of the fish's mouth.'

Gib swallowed hard, then started the lift again, sending it up to the children's ICU. The doors opened on three policemen huddled around a third figure.

'Lisa!' The man fell into the arms of the woman they were escorting, and she held him close, then, ignoring the police, she led him back into the ICU, crying brokenly while he now soothed and comforted her.

Resisting an urge to rearrange the features of the insensitive oaf who'd approached the delicate subject of organ donation so brutally, Gib made his way back to his own domain.

Sophie sat on the floor of the child-care centre, Thomas on her knee, her arms clasped around him, her mind not on the story Vicki was reading in an attempt to restore normality to the group but on Gib's words.

But no matter how she twisted them, they still made no sense.

She should have phoned Paula and sorted out the paternity thing once and for all, but she'd been wrapped in a selfish little cloud of bliss, wanting only for today to come so she and Gib could progress to the next stage of their relationship.

He'd said 'my son'. It *had* to mean something.

She did the sums again. Thomas was just over three so

he'd been conceived four years ago. Would a man who'd still been wearing his wedding ring four years after his wife's death have had an affair with Hilary either just before or just after that death?

Unlikely!

And where would they have met?

Medicine and science crossed paths often, but Hilary wasn't the kind of person who would have rushed into an affair.

Surely not with a man whose wife was ill.

But what if it *had* happened that way, and what if Gillian had found out, and what if…?

Would that explain the guilt Gib felt about her death?

The thought made Sophie want to cry.

Thomas, not in the least concerned about the drama that had been played out, eased himself out of her arms and took off to play with a friend, and Sophie stood up. Enough useless speculation. She'd phone Paula.

Right now!

Not from her office but from one of the public phones in the foyer.

She said goodbye to Thomas, borrowed some change from the centre manager, who was sitting, still shaky, in her office, then made the call.

'Paula, I know this will seem like a strange question, but was Hilary friendly with any particular man at the institute?'

'Only Gib, but you'd know that, having seen him at the service. As you know, she was a very private person, but I'd say if she talked to anyone about anything, it would have been Gib.'

The words resounded meaninglessly in Sophie's suddenly empty head, and her stomach lurched with physical denial.

'Gib?' she managed at last. 'My Gib?'

He wasn't her Gib but Paula apparently knew what she meant.

'Alexander Gibson from the NICU,' she clarified. 'Didn't you know he worked here for some years? His wife was sick and he needed a job with regular hours so he could care for her at night. I think he had a carer living in for the daytime. We were working on genetic links with pre-term births and he has a science degree as well as his medical one, and his specialty was neonates, so it was a terrific fit. He worked alongside Hilary so naturally they'd have grown close.'

Naturally they'd have grown close?

He had a sick wife! Sophie wanted to yell into the phone, as hopes and dreams came crashing down around her.

'Thanks, Paula,' she managed, but Paula wasn't appeased by the simple words and asked why Sophie needed to know.

Sophie scrabbled around in her devastated mind.

'Hilary left something that could be his.'

It had been intended as an excuse, but even as Sophie said goodbye the horrible truth of the statement struck her so forcibly she shuddered.

Thomas could be his child.

Not only that, but if he wanted to claim him, he already had a built-in carer for him.

My son! he'd said, less than an hour earlier.

He knew!

And hadn't said anything to her?

Sophie sighed and rested her head against the plastic privacy bubble that surrounded the phone.

She'd fallen in love with her sister's lover.

And if that wasn't bad enough, he wasn't the man she'd thought him. He obviously hadn't loved Hilary because he'd cravenly refused to have anything to do with her child.

He'd taken advantage of Hilary's feelings for him, betrayed his wife—or her memory—then denied his own child.

Bleak black clouds of despair hovered in Sophie's head, while her heart wept blood for the love that might have been.

But he wouldn't get Thomas! No man who could be so callous was going to have her beloved child.

Confused and terrified, she searched for a solution.

Not that there was any choice. She had to see Gib. Had to demand to know what had gone on in the past—and what was going on in his mind now.

Fear gave way to anger as she made her way back up to the NICU, where she was relieved to find it was quiet, and no nurses were demanding she look at this baby or that.

Then she remembered she'd last seen Gib disappearing into a lift with a man who'd had a knife, and, in spite of her anger, her heart stopped beating.

'Is Gib back?' Dry lips formed the question, directed to the nearest nurse, who tilted her head in the direction of his office.

Sophie charged towards it, manners dispensed with as she barged straight in.

'Sophie? Are you all right? Is Thomas OK? The other kids?'

He stood up and came towards her, putting his hands on her shoulders and looking searchingly into her face.

Her resolve weakened, though she knew she should be strong, so it took a mammoth effort to pull away from those comforting hands and confront the man who had just destroyed her happiness.

'You said "my son"!' she said, her voice rising as anger won the battle with desire. 'What makes you think Thomas is your son? Because you had an affair with my sister? Is that it? While you were married to an ill woman, or did you wait until Gillian died? I saw you at the service and I thought you were there because you cared for me and had somehow found out about it but, no, you were there for Hilary—for the woman who bore the son you didn't want to acknowledge. I can't believe it. I can't understand it. Not you, or Hilary's behaviour, or anyone not wanting to have contact with their child, not any of it. Not even how you knew. And worst of all that you knew and didn't tell me! Here I've been, organising a memorial service so I could find Thomas's father, and he's right there under my nose the whole time, only too cowardly to tell me—too cowardly to want a child.'

The angst and anger had flowed out with the words, leaving Sophie suddenly depleted, so she wasn't sure what to do next.

She'd wanted answers but now she didn't want to hear them—didn't want to know her sister and this man had been lovers.

Didn't want to know anything!

She turned to walk away but he caught her and swung her around so she was all but in his arms.

Her body ached to rest against his—to be held close to him until all the pain and rage subsided—but that would be fatal and her mind retained enough working brain cells to know it, so she pushed away from him again and left the room, hearing his urgent 'Sophie, we must talk,' but refusing to heed it.

'Mistletoe!' Albert greeted her as she returned to the ward. He was holding a sprig of plastic greenery in the air above her head and kissed her soundly on the lips.

Someone applauded and she turned to see Gib standing not far behind her. A nurse snatched the mistletoe from Albert and held it over Gib's head, kissing him then twirling away and kissing Albert before heading towards the foyer in search of other men to kiss.

Albert caught Gib's attention and the pair went over to the new baby's crib, discussing, from what Sophie could hear of the conversation, whether the little girl could go home. Normally she would go into the intermediate ward, where babies with slight problems following their birth were kept for a few days, but being Christmas...

Sophie sighed, then looked around. The young paediatrician was here, Gib was here, she was working on Christmas Day so logically she was due some extra time off.

She'd collect Thomas early and take him to the park. She'd get some bread and they'd feed the ducks and then they'd go and get a burger and stay there for a very long time.

Yes, she wanted some answers from Gib—just not tonight, not when it was meant to be their special night together.

'Oh, Sophie, have you seen Mackenzie?' Maria's question put paid to her plans—as if she could have left anyway, when her job was here.

'Not since this morning,' she replied, following Maria to Mackenzie's crib.

'Look!' Maria said, and Sophie saw the little girl lying with her eyes wide open, turning towards Maria as she murmured her daughter's name.

Smiling?

Not possible, but no way Sophie was going to dampen Maria's joy by mentioning wind.

Anyway, maybe it was a smile—as she and Gib had once agreed, miracles did happen.

Gib!

'I fed her this morning, just a little after I'd expressed my milk, and she's not showing any reaction—isn't that great?'

'It's wonderful,' Sophie agreed, her nerve-endings twitching to attention as Gib approached.

'It is indeed,' he said, standing so close to Sophie she wanted to howl in protest. Or move away. But she was trapped between the crib and the man behind her.

'And Carly, Kristie and Angus are all doing well. I was surprised at how quickly their bilirubin levels dropped. Well done, Sophie, for starting the phototherapy so early.'

'I was following accepted protocols,' she snapped, not wanting his praise, not wanting him close to her.

'Accepted protocols don't always help us, though, because situations differ. A bit like promises.'

He walked away, his shoulder lightly brushing against Sophie's back as he turned.

'What's he talking about?' Maria asked.

'Who knows?' Sophie muttered, then added an angry 'Who cares?' under her breath, although she knew the answer to that one.

She did.

But now she was in the nursery, she moved on to see the babies who'd had phototherapy. Helen was nursing Angus, holding the little boy against her breast, while Dan had his big hand resting in the crib with the other two.

'I know I can do this in the special room,' Helen said

apologetically, 'but he feeds so much better if he's near his sisters.'

'He's a funny wee scrap, isn't he?' Sophie said, looking down into the angelic pink face and the little red lips sucking greedily at his mother's breast. 'Do you think it's a macho thing? That he feels responsible for his sisters?'

'More likely he's got used to his sisters looking out for him.'

This time she hadn't heard—or felt—Gib approach, although this time he was wheeling the crib with Baby Neilsen in it, so maybe that had cut off the vibes.

'My sisters have always believed I was their responsibility—still do, though we're all over forty. Poor Angus, he's got a lifetime of being bossed by females ahead of him.'

This was normal NICU chat—the stuff that went on all the time when no one was in crisis. Even during crises, at times. But how could Gib do it? How could he be so unconcerned when the—what, love?—that had been building between them had blown up in their faces?

'If everything's under control, I might leave now,' she managed to say, reverting to her earlier idea of getting out of the place.

'Go right ahead. Thomas could probably do with some extra mothering.'

She spun towards him, wanting to yell at him again, to tell him not to use Thomas's name, but his blue eyes were burning into hers—telling her things she didn't understand. Telling her everything would be all right...

How?

She turned away, then heard his voice, introducing Baby Neilsen to Maria and Helen and Dan.

'This is Alexander John Neilsen,' he said, and Sophie

had to smile. Baby Neilsen finally had a name; Carly, Kristie and Angus were over their jaundice; Mackenzie was showing no ill effects from enteral feeding—Christmas joy was flooding through the NICU.

Flooding through the child-care centre as well, she realised when Thomas pushed stars and cards and a crushed-looking present into her hands.

'For under the tree. Did you know Santa puts presents under the tree, Sophie? And we can put presents there as well. Can we put a present there for Aunt Etty? And for Gib?'

She chose to ignore the last question.

'I've got a present for you to give to Aunt Etty,' she assured him.

'And one for Gib? I like Gib.'

Only because Gib could lift him on his shoulders, and could throw him into the water with a huge splash.

She pushed the ungracious thoughts aside.

'What do you think Gib might like?' she asked.

'Chocolate elephants,' Thomas announced, so certain of the choice Sophie could only stare at him.

'Because I know he likes chocolate, Aunt Etty told me, and he knows I like elephants because he read me the elephant story, so we could give him chocolate elephants and he might share.'

Three-year-old logic, was Sophie's first thought, but the second one, following close on its heels, was a question.

'When did Gib read you the elephant story?'

'When he put me to bed.'

They were at the car, and conversation ceased while she buckled him into his seat, but at least Sophie had one answer. He'd seen the photo of Hilary by Thomas's bed and done the sums.

But hadn't told her.

And Thomas wanted her to buy chocolate elephants as a gift?

They fed the ducks, wandered through the park, had dinner at McDonald's, then hired some DVDs from the video store and went home. Thomas was asleep in the car by the time they arrived.

Sophie changed him and tucked him into bed, then, not wanting to run into Gib, she phoned Etty and asked if she'd be around for an hour or so.

'Last-minute shopping,' Sophie explained, wondering if there were such things as chocolate elephants and assuming if there were, then the chocolate shop in the big local shopping centre would have them.

'Just turn the monitor on,' Etty said, 'and when you get back, why don't you come in and have a Christmas drink with me?'

Just you? Sophie wanted to ask, but she couldn't.

'I don't think so,' she said to Etty. 'It's been a big day. On top of the normal Christmas stuff happening in the hospital, we had a drama at the child-care centre. Early night for me. I'll give you a buzz on the monitor when I get back.'

She left the flat by the outside door, relieved to get away. She wanted answers from Gib, but she was too distressed to handle them right now. Too hurt, and confused, and, yes, still too angry.

CHAPTER TEN

HE WAS sitting on her doorstep when she returned, and no avoidance tactic would work.

'Finished your shopping?'

Sophie held up the bag she was carrying.

'Would you believe it's a present for you from Thomas? From the son you didn't want to know.'

'If he is my son,' Gib said quietly, standing up but not approaching her.

'What do you mean by that?' Sophie demanded. 'If you're implying my sister slept around, I'll—I'll—'

'Kick my teeth in?' he said helpfully, making Sophie even more furious than she already was.

'Something like that!' she seethed.

'Sophie, Hilary didn't sleep around. She didn't even sleep with me.'

'Oh, no? Pregnancy by osmosis, was it?'

'Pregnancy by donor—all I did was give some sperm to Hilary.'

'You were a sperm donor?' The notion was too much to take in, Sophie's mind scrambling to find purchase in it. 'But that's anonymous—the donors are anonymous—and you said "my son".'

'It's not anonymous when you do it for a friend,' Gib said quietly, then, apparently realising Sophie had got beyond the teeth-kicking stage, he stepped towards her.

'Let's sit. I'll explain. Do you want to go down by the river?'

Down by the river? With moonlight and lapping water? She mightn't be as angry now, but she wasn't insane.

'No!'

'Then we'll sit on the step.'

He didn't touch her, merely stood aside so she could reach the step, which wasn't, when he sat down as well, nearly big enough for two people, especially when one of them didn't want to be touching the other.

'Hilary wanted a child,' he began, his sombre tones suggesting the memories he was dredging up were painful. 'I don't know if she ever talked to you about it, but she talked to me, I guess because we were friends. Then one day she asked me if I'd donate sperm.'

Sophie's heart, which had been beating erratically since she'd seen Gib on the step, now slowed to snail pace, while the pain she heard in Gib's voice flowed along her nerves.

'How could I give her a child when I hadn't had one with Gillian?' he whispered. 'I said no, and that was that. Then Gillian died—died the way she did—and it was as if my whole world tilted off its axis. I was so hurt that she would do that to me, hurting that I'd lost her and angry with myself that somehow I should have known and stopped her. I know grief is always terrible to bear, but mine wasn't clean grief, Sophie, it wasn't even healthy grief. Can you understand that?'

She could and slid her hand across to touch his knee because the lump in her throat prevented speech.

'I went back to the institute to finalise what I'd been doing before starting back at the NICU and found Hilary was nearly as miserable as I was. Her beloved grandmother had died and she was devastated, finally resigning, saying she was going back to Sydney to live with her sister.'

He covered Sophie's hand with his, and gently squeezed her fingers.

'You?'

Sophie nodded in the dark and waited, needing to hear it all.

'She was grieving or I doubt she'd have said anything, but when I said goodbye to her she asked me again. She told me how desperate she was to have a child, and with her grandmother's inheritance would even have had the resources to take five years off work to devote to her child until he or she went to school.'

He paused again, while an image of Hilary, crying as she'd boarded the plane to return to Brisbane after Gran's funeral, flashed through Sophie's head.

So unhappy, it had broken Sophie's heart!

'Anyway,' Gib continued, 'suddenly it made no sense that we should both be so unhappy, especially if there was some way I could perhaps bring her just some hope of joy. So I said I'd do it, but guilt still nagged at me—the guilt of making a child with someone other than Gillian. So, because of that, and out of respect for her memory, I told Hilary I didn't want to know if she conceived. She promised me she wouldn't reveal who the father was and that she'd make no claims on me. And in return I promised I would never tell my part of it or ever make a claim on the child.'

There was a long pause before he added two more words. 'Not ever!'

'So when you read the elephant story and saw Hilary's photo…?'

Sophie couldn't finish the sentence, but she didn't object when Gib put his arm around her shoulder and tugged her closer.

'I didn't know what to do! To say I was gobsmacked— well, that doesn't start to describe it. What were the odds of the two of us meeting? Of the child I didn't know I had actually living under my roof? And to make matters worse, there was this woman who'd come into my life, bringing all the laughter and sunshine I hadn't realised I'd been missing, and to add to my fears about failing her as I'd failed Gillian, I now discover the child she loves might just be my own.'

He held her against his body and stared into the darkness.

'Should I have told you?'

Sophie stared into the darkness, searching for answer.

Was there one?

'I don't know,' she said, while she tried to sort through all the things she'd heard. It was like putting a jigsaw puzzle together, fitting all the sky pieces but setting aside bits that didn't fit.

'The odds of our meeting weren't that enormous,' she said carefully, because, in spite of what he'd said about laughter and sunshine, he hadn't mentioned love. 'Yes, that I ended up working for you *is* a coincidence, and our living together stems from that, but I came to Brisbane to find you.'

Gib tightened his arm around her shoulders and wondered how she'd react if he dropped just a small kiss on her cheek.

He tried it, and when she didn't hit him, he found the breath to repeat her words back to her.

'You came to Brisbane to find me?'

She turned and pressed her lips to his cheek this time.

'To find Thomas's father,' she explained. 'That's why I had the memorial service. Well, Hilary's friend Paula had suggested it, and I went along with it so I could check out the men Hilary had worked with. It seemed as good a place as any to begin.'

Gib shook his head.

'If that was all you wanted to do, why take a job here? Couldn't you have flown up, stayed a couple of weeks then gone back to Sydney?'

'I...'

He felt her stiffen and turned her in his arms, holding her close, wondering what it was that she found so hard to talk about.

'I thought once his father knew about him, he might want to keep in touch, and it would be easier if we were in Brisbane. Thomas is a little boy—I thought one day he might need his father.'

Gib groaned as he processed the hoarsely whispered words. How could he *not* have considered that when he'd made his promise to Hilary?

He drew Sophie closer and kissed her cheek.

'You did this on the off-chance a selfish man might one day realise the full extent of his selfishness? You left your home town and friends and family, and came up here for Thomas?'

He felt her shiver then edge away from him, shaking her head.

'Don't give me too much credit,' she said. 'I definitely had an ulterior motive for finding Thomas's father. It wasn't until after I'd decided I had to find him that I thought about the other stuff—about maybe being able to keep in touch.'

'You *had* to find him?' Gib probed.

A long soft sigh carried through the darkness towards him.

'Did Hilary tell you much about our family?'

Gib shook his head then realised Sophie wouldn't see the gesture in the darkness, so spoke as well.

'She was a very private person,' he said quietly. 'I think maybe you are, too.'

Another sigh, then the woman he knew he loved crept closer, leaning against him, so it was only natural he'd put his arms around her.

'Everyone talks about their dysfunctional families, and I know really horrible things happen to children, and plenty of people would say our family was fine, but there was no love, Gib, and children can't be reared without love.'

He tucked her closer, and squeezed her shoulder, waiting for this so private woman to dredge up a past she had put behind her.

'I didn't know Hilary's father, but he was obviously just another of my mother's enthusiasms. That's what men were to her—enthusiasms. She'd grab one and totally focus on him to the exclusion of all else, then tire of him and he'd be discarded.'

'But her children?'

'Mistakes! Oh, she might have thought she wanted children, but she had no time for them at all. She paid for care for us, and that was that. I cannot remember one kiss my mother ever gave me, nor a hug, nor even a dressing-down for being naughty. And I *was* naughty.'

Sophie paused, feeling the pain of those years when

she'd tried everything her small child's mind could think of to attract the attention of the woman she'd adored.

'She was beautiful, and carefree, always laughing—or so it seemed to me—with kisses and hugs for the men who came and went. Some, like my father and Hilary's and the stuffed-shirt she's with now, she married, but in between there were plenty more. Hilary was only four years older than me, but she became my mother. I don't know if it was instinct, or if at some time one of my mother's men had abused her, but when I was about three she put me in my stroller and we ran away for the first time. We always went to Gran's and we were always taken back, but Hilary never gave up and Gran realised something was very wrong for her to keep doing it, so when I was five she started court proceedings. It took a long time, because I was eight and Hilary was twelve before Gran was appointed our legal guardian and we went to live with her. Gran was wonderful, but I think by then it was too late for Hilary to learn about love and affection and how a hug is sometimes all you need. She knew it worked for other people, for she'd hugged and kissed me all her life, but somehow she felt it couldn't be that way for her.'

Gib stared into the darkness, seeing the two children who had gone through their formative years without love, understanding the reserved woman he had known at the institute and why the only way she could ever have had the child she longed for had been in the way they'd done it.

And understanding why Sophie had wanted someone free with hugs and kisses to help her care for Hilary's child. Thomas would never suffer from a deprivation of love.

Thomas?

'And Thomas? Finding his father?'

'My mother wants him.' Fear reverberated in the dry words, hurting Gib because there was pain behind them as well. 'I think it was to do with image that she fought to keep Hilary and me. Her friends all had children who were put on display from time to time, so she had to have some, too. Her latest husband is some wealthy politician who seems to think bringing up a step-grandchild will be good for his image so my mother has started court proceedings. I'm single, I work long hours, I have to put Thomas into child care—she knows all the angles and has plenty of money to fight her case.'

'Ah!' Gib said as the rest of the pieces of the puzzle fell into place. 'So you had to find Thomas's father to get his support for you to keep the little boy.'

Sophie nodded in the darkness, suddenly exhausted.

Had Gib sensed it, that he kissed her lightly on the head and said 'Go to bed'?

Go to bed? That's all?

But she was too tired to argue, and probably too tired to put much effort into the kisses she thought she'd have preferred. She let him help her to her feet and lead her into the flat, picking up her parcel and handing it to her as he gently kissed her goodnight outside her bedroom door.

She cupped her palm against his cheek and looked into his eyes, catching the glimmer of a smile lurking there.

'You look pleased with yourself,' she said. 'What are you up to?'

He bent his head and kissed her again.

'I'm going to postpone Christmas,' he said. 'But first I have to get to the shops before they shut, then make a million phone calls. Go to bed. I'll see you in the morning.'

None of it made sense so Sophie did as she was told and went to bed.

* * *

The next day was a work day, nothing more, Sophie realised as she woke to find Thomas standing by her bed, his eyes fixed anxiously on her face.

'Is it Christmas yet?' he asked. 'Can we look under the tree?'

'One more sleep,' she said, because she couldn't bear that he'd have this first Christmas when it meant something to him without her. 'I have to go to work, and you'll stay with Aunt Etty and—'

She was about to say Etty would take him to a party, but Gib's strange remark about postponing Christmas popped into her head and she held back, wondering what on earth it meant.

'One more sleep?' Thomas checked, as he and his elephant climbed into bed with her and snuggled up against her.

'That's all,' she promised, then she drew him into her arms and kissed him, kissing him all over until his giggling and squirming made her stop.

What next? she wondered as he in turn pressed giggling kisses on his elephant. She and Gib had talked and all the pieces of the puzzle were finally in place, but he'd made no commitment about Thomas—or towards her, although she could hardly expect that of him.

Yet, she thought wistfully as she got out of bed and hustled Thomas through to the kitchen for his breakfast, it would be such a simple solution—she and Gib could marry and that way he'd be twice Thomas's father.

She shivered at the thought, not with delight but because she knew that fairy-tales rarely came true.

With Thomas washed and dressed, she phoned Etty to ask if she'd play along with the one-more-sleep scenario. Etty agreed, and it was only when Sophie added 'So if you take him to Gib's family party, could you tell him it's a Christmas Eve party?' that Etty seemed a little taken aback.

'Of course,' she said, but Sophie could hear doubt in her voice. Before she could wonder what was going on, Thomas tugged at her skirt, ready to get on with his day. She took him through to the house and handed him over to Etty, who announced they were going to make gingerbread men.

'Gingerbread men?' Thomas echoed, wonderment in his voice and adoration in his eyes as he looked up at the woman who brought such magic to his life.

'That's right,' Etty said briskly. 'Now, kiss Sophie good-bye and we'll get started.'

Sophie smiled to herself as she drove to work. She sometimes wondered if she should be jealous of the love Thomas felt for Etty, but she never felt anything but gratitude and relief that Gib had made that particular arrangement possible. It was perfect, and Sophie knew that whatever happened between herself and Gib, Etty would always be there for Thomas.

'Santa hat for you,' Sally greeted her, when she reached the ward. As everyone in the hospital seemed to be wearing Santa hats, Sophie accepted hers with good grace.

So it was a day that started well, and continued that way. It was quiet in the unit. The new baby had gone home, Alexander John Neilsen had moved into the intermediate unit and Carly, Kristie and Angus, no longer needing monitoring, were in one of the family rooms with their mum and dad.

Sophie took advantage of the peace and slipped up to the ICU. Marty must have had the same idea as she was there, not counting foetal heartbeats but talking to the baby, telling it about Christmas.

'Couldn't resist?' she teased Sophie, and Sophie smiled,

admitting that she felt the woman and her unborn child deserved more than to be left alone on Christmas Day. Marty slipped away but Sophie stayed a while, holding the woman's unresponsive hand and singing quietly to the baby.

Back in the unit little had changed.

'It must be the Christmas spirit that's made them all better this week,' Maria said, nursing a sleeping Mackenzie in her arms.

'It must be,' Sophie agreed, as a disturbance in the foyer made them both turn. A group of carol singers stood there, shuffling into order, their leader stepping forward to explain he knew they had to sing quietly here, and if they did, would it be OK?

'Go right ahead,' Sophie told them, and all the staff stopped what they were doing and turned to listen to the carols, Sophie looking at Maria and realising she and Mackenzie were symbolic of all the mothers and babies who came through this place. It had been a battle but eventually little Mackenzie would go home, where with the love and attention of her family she would thrive.

Family?

Apart from Gran and Hilary, it had been an alien concept to Sophie.

Up till now?

Could it happen?

Could she and Gib and Thomas become a family?

She hardly dared to hope—knowing Gib's reservations, understanding them.

The singers segued into 'Silent Night' and Sophie forgot about Gib and thought only of her sister—of Hilary, who had taught her how to love.

* * *

Gib wasn't sure how he'd done it, but by midnight on Christmas Eve he'd managed to pull it all together. He slept in on Christmas morning, at times hearing Thomas's chatter as background noise but dozing off again without it disturbing him.

Tonight he'd talk to Sophie, then tomorrow…

He smiled to himself as he walked through the house, finding Thomas with Etty in the kitchen and asking him if he'd like a swim.

The little boy ran so happily—so trustingly—towards him, Gib felt his heart tighten with an emotion he'd never felt before. He swung Thomas into his arms and hugged him, sure this child must be the greatest Christmas gift a man could ever receive.

Although there was one more he'd like…

Sophie arrived home late, the staff going off duty insisting she have a Christmas drink with them, plying her with lemonade when she'd refused champagne.

Thomas was already in bed, asleep.

'He was exhausted, poor wee lad,' Etty explained.

'I'm feeling a bit that way myself,' Sophie told her, then remembered her manners. 'Did you have a good day? Enjoy the Christmas party?'

Etty frowned at her.

'But we're having Christmas tomorrow,' Etty reminded her, and Sophie was too tired to do anything but agree. She'd have liked to ask where Gib was, but guessed he was still visiting his family, and though disappointment shafted through her, she said goodnight to Etty and headed into the flat. She'd been eating Christmas goodies all day at the hospital—a cup of tea and some toast would be all she needed for dinner, then she'd go to bed.

Alone.

She was just drifting off to sleep when she remembered she hadn't put Thomas's presents under the tree. She got up, pulled a light robe over her nightgown, found the stash in the bottom of her cupboard and tiptoed out of the flat.

The coloured lights flickering on the tree lit the room enough for her to make her way quietly towards it, but it wasn't until she bent down to place her parcels beneath it that she realised she wasn't alone.

'I was wondering if you'd remember,' Gib said quietly. 'Etty said you were very tired and I didn't know if I should sneak into the flat and find them and put them under the tree for you.'

That was it? He was sitting in the flickering light, wondering about putting parcels under the tree?

Sophie sighed. She'd misread the signals between them. In spite of what his kisses had said to her, he'd obviously meant what he'd said about not wanting a permanent involvement with anyone.

But they worked together—and they'd share Thomas—she'd still see him…

Cold comfort when what she'd really wanted was a Christmas miracle.

'Everything OK at work?'

The question confirmed her gloomy thoughts.

'Very OK,' she said, backing away from the tree—backing away from Gib lest she hurl herself into his arms and beg him to love her.

'Can I get you something?'

This was too much! She felt an urge to pick up the nearest present and hurl it at him, but he was still talking in that quiet, emotionless voice.

'Cup of tea? Brandy? Champagne? Engagement ring?'

'*What* did you say?'

'Cup of tea—'

She *would* throw something at him.

'I didn't mean that bit,' she snapped, and heard him chuckle.

'Come and sit by me. I've been trying to do this without us touching because we both know where that can lead and I'm sure, tonight of all nights, you need to be sleeping near Thomas, but I need you close while I tell you how I love you. Was it Shakespeare who said, "Let me count the ways"? I couldn't begin to count with you, Sophie. You came into my life and it was as if you lit it from within, helping me out of the dark places I'd been inhabiting for too long.'

She took two tentative steps towards him and he reached out and took her hand, pulling her down beside him.

'You brought something new—something I'd never felt before, or if I had, I'd forgotten it. You brought contentment and if that doesn't sound like something wonderful, believe me when I say it's the most beautiful gift in the world.'

He put his hand on her chin and turned her head, dropping a light kiss on her lips.

'I love you, Sophie. Will you marry me?'

Sophie stared at him, watching his face turn blue then green then red in the blinking lights.

'You don't want to get involved,' she reminded him.

'I didn't,' he corrected her, 'until a tall, slim woman with long black hair and a smile that could light up the universe came into my life and hauled me back into the land of the living. You brought my body back to life with the attraction that flared between us, but more than that you eased away the pain and guilt and endless questions that have tortured me for years. You made me whole again, Sophie, and that's another gift because you deserve the best and nothing but a whole man would be good enough for you.'

She snuggled against him, aware of the danger, knowing he was right—she needed to be in her own bed whenever an excited Thomas woke up for Christmas—but needing to feel close to Gib while she tried to absorb all that he had said.

'It's your turn to talk,' he whispered, dropping kisses, as he often did, on her hair, splaying it out with his fingers at the same time, tugging lightly at it as he played with it.

'I don't know what to say,' she whispered.

'Perhaps you could tell me you love me,' he coached, and she could hear a little fear as well as laughter in his voice.

'You already know that,' she said. 'I've told you that with kisses.'

'But I need to hear the words,' he persisted, so she said them.

She said, 'I love you Gib,' then had to quell a strong desire to shout them loudly—to go to the window and yell them down the river.

'So will you marry me?'

'I will,' she said, quietly, the strength of this commitment stealing her breath.

'So, one Christmas present for the lady. You're allowed to open one on Christmas Eve—our Christmas Eve.'

He pressed a small box into her hands, and she opened it with shaking fingers, seeing the diamond nestled there, square cut, seeming huge, winking like the Christmas lights at her.

'Try it on,' Gib said, the hoarseness of his voice telling her he was as shaken by this moment as she was.

'You do it,' she said, and held out a trembling hand, trying to hold it steady while he placed the ring on her finger.

'Next time I do that you'll be Mrs Gibson,' he murmured, then he kissed her and they didn't talk for a long, long time.

'Now is it Christmas?'

Sophie unglued sticky eyelids and looked into the hopeful eyes of the child and the black button eyes of the elephant.

'Yes, today is Christmas,' she told Thomas, and watched his face light up with excitement. 'Just let me get up and get dressed and then I'll help you get dressed and we'll go and see if Santa left you something under the tree.'

Santa had, and the next hour passed in a welter of excitement as Thomas tore wrappings off presents, then showed them excitedly to Sophie, Aunt Etty and Gib.

'See you've got a nice present yourself,' Etty said quietly, as she passed Sophie a cup of coffee.

Sophie felt a blush creeping up her cheeks, and when she opened her mouth all she could do was stammer.

'Don't bother explaining. I knew from the moment I saw you that you were the best thing that ever happened to him,' Etty said calmly. 'I'm just pleased he realised it.'

With all his presents opened, Thomas then became a tiny Santa, passing presents to Etty and Gib, waiting excitedly while Gib opened his chocolate elephants then dancing with delight when Gib assured him they were just what he'd wanted.

They ate a light breakfast of seasonal fruit and pancakes, then Gib announced it was time to get going.

'Going where?' Sophie asked, and Gib smiled at her.

'To meet the family, of course.'

'Your family?' Sophie said, certain he'd told her they celebrated Christmas on the actual day.

'My family,' he confirmed. 'They put it off until today so I could bring them something special.'

He lifted Thomas in his arms, settled him on his hip, then put his free arm around Sophie.

'What could be more special than my new wife-to-be and son?' he said, and Sophie saw the love he felt for both of them shining in his eyes, and knew that this was what she had always wanted. A real family.

MILLS & BOON®

Live the emotion

_MedicaL
romance™

THE SURGEON'S MIRACLE BABY
by Carol Marinelli

Consultant surgeon Daniel Ashwood has come to
Australia to find the woman he loved and lost a year
ago. Unfortunately he is currently Louise Andrews's
patient. Nevertheless, he is determined to see if she
will give their relationship anther try. But Louise has
a surprise for him – a three-month-old surprise!

A CONSULTANT CLAIMS HIS BRIDE
by Maggie Kingsley

Consultant Jonah Washington is Nurse Manager
Nell Sutherland's rock – and her best friend. Let
down by another man, Nell begins to realise how
wonderful Jonah really is. She is shocked by her
changed reaction to him – why had she never
realised before just how irresistible the gorgeous
consultant is?

THE WOMAN HE'S BEEN WAITING FOR
by Jennifer Taylor

Playboy doctor Harry Shaw is rich, successful, and
extremely handsome. Since his arrival at Ferndale
Surgery he has charmed almost everybody – except
GP Grace Kennedy. Grace refuses to be impressed
by Harry's charisma and looks – she has known him
too long! But Grace hasn't counted on her heart
completely over-ruling her head...

On sale 5th January 2007

*Available at WHSmith, Tesco, ASDA, Borders, Eason,
Sainsbury's and most bookshops*

www.millsandboon.co.uk

1206/03a

Unwrap three gorgeous men this holiday season!

For three women, the Christmas holidays bring more than just festive cheer – even as they try to escape the holiday celebrations and forget about absent partners or failed relationships.

What they don't realise is that you can't escape love, especially at Christmas time...

On sale 17th November 2006

www.millsandboon.co.uk

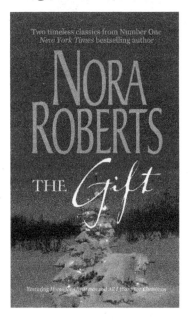

FREE!

4 Books
and a surprise gift!

We would like to take this opportunity to thank you for reading this Mills & Boon® book by offering you the chance to take FOUR more specially selected titles from the Medical Romance™ series absolutely FREE! We're also making this offer to introduce you to the benefits of the Mills & Boon® Reader Service™—

- ★ **FREE home delivery**
- ★ **FREE gifts and competitions**
- ★ **FREE monthly Newsletter**
- ★ **Exclusive Reader Service offers**
- ★ **Books available before they're in the shops**

Accepting these FREE books and gift places you under no obligation to buy. you may cancel at any time. even after receiving your free shipment. Simply complete your details below and return the entire page to the address below. You don't even need a stamp!

YES! Please send me 4 free Medical Romance books and a surprise gift. I understand that unless you hear from me. I will receive 6 superb new titles every month for just £2.80 each. postage and packing free. I am under no obligation to purchase any books and may cancel my subscription at any time. The free books and gift will be mine to keep in any case.

M6ZEF

Ms/Mrs/Miss/Mr ....Initials....................................

BLOCK CAPITALS PLEASE

Surname ....

Address...

....

....Postcode ....

Send this whole page to:
UK: FREEPOST CN81, Croydon, CR9 3WZ